AUSTRALIAN
QUINOLOGY

Five Australian Novels of Our Way of Life

HOWARD REEDE-PELLING

Order this book online at www.trafford.com
or email orders@trafford.com

Most Trafford titles are also available at major online book retailers.

Print information available on the last page.

ISBN: 978-1-4907-6208-1 (sc)
ISBN: 978-1-4907-6207-4 (e)

Because of the dynamic nature of the Internet, any web addresses or links contained in
this book may have changed since publication and may no longer be valid. The views
expressed in this work are solely those of the author and do not necessarily reflect the
views of the publisher, and the publisher hereby disclaims any responsibility for them.

Any people depicted in stock imagery provided by Thinkstock are models,
and such images are being used for illustrative purposes only.
Certain stock imagery © Thinkstock.

Trafford rev.   09/14/2016

 www.trafford.com

North America & international
toll-free: 1 888 232 4444 (USA & Canada)
fax: 812 355 4082

Index

Australian Quinology by © Howard Reede-Pelling.

These five stories depict a sordid way of life and are unsuitable for **junior readers.** The writings contain references to sex, drugs and violence. Unseemly language is also heavily used throughout the five tales.

Adult readers only are encouraged to enjoy these manuscripts.

Bernie is an exercise in an adult way of life with teenagers.

Exit the Cross has the seedy style of the old King's Cross in Sydney depicted, with Pimps, Male and Female Prostitutes, Bad Language, Drugs and Violence.

Pat-Tricia is the story of two eight year old girls who are mixed up at the airport. One goes to a nice family and the other to a Prostitute. This tale is how the two girls coped.

Laurie is a relation of two no-hopers who have not grown up yet, they are typical of many young people nowadays who just take rather than give; as is the norm with a great majority of down and out people.

Gold Digger How a street girl is transformed into a lady. Drugs, violence and unseemly language mixed with high society.

**No intention is made to people alive or
deceased in any of the above writings.**

Illustrations

Book One :   **Australian Trilogy**
                Three illustrations by **Fay Salmon.**

Book Two :   **Australian Quinology**
                Five illustrations by her daughter **B. O' L.**

Bernie

This story covers the troubles of some teenagers and a love triangle which comes to a scuffle that eventually concerns the police. Drugs are mentioned and foul language is present, this tale is not suitable for minors and is r-rated. This tale is entirely fictional and no intention is made towards people alive or deceased.

Bernie   © Howard Reede-Pelling

Bernie ducked the vicious right cross, took the soft left feint on his right forearm which he used to block and with blurring speed and deadly accuracy, followed in with a shattering straight left that smashed the already bloody nose of the chunky half-wit that dared to take him on. A smart follow-up right cross of his own had his assailant on his back at Doris' feet. She gasped at the sight of all the blood frothing from the fallen man's swollen face. Bernie was very little marked himself, only a pinkish lump where his jaw was swollen, gave evidence that 'Sharkey' had hit him at all. As Sharkey Dramford slowly eased himself up, Bernie moved in ready to dish out more of the same; his chin tucked in to the left shoulder, right guard waving in readiness. Sharkey raised both hands palms outward signifying he'd had enough, which was a trick to catch Bernie off-guard, for Sharkey swung a vicious kick at Bernie's balls. However, Bernie was ready for some such move and grabbed the offending leg, pulling it upwards as high as he could. Sharkey's other foot was lifted clear of the ground and his head fell back, hitting the pavement with a resounding thud. He lay still.

"Oh my God, Bernie - you've killed him!" Doris gasped.

Bernie thought he had too. He put his ear to the fallen man's chest.

"No, I can feel his heart beating, I think he's just unconscious - serves the bastard right!"

"We'll have to get the Doctor to him Bernie." Doris was worried he might bleed to death.

Bernie snarled.

"Nah! Bugger him - he brought it on himself." Then. "Yair, s'pose we'd better!"

He sat Sharkey against the wall and made sure his breathing passages were clear, then wiping the blood from his fingers to the victim's already soiled clothing; he took Doris

3

by the arm and hurried off to a telephone box. The operator wanted details but Bernie just told him where the unconscious body lay and hung up. Over a can of coke and a sandwich, Bernie eyed Doris; taking her clothes off mentally. The way she was appraising him, he thought, she was probably doing the same thing.

"He might die." She stated, matter-of-factly.

"Serves the prick right!"

"It'd be manslaughter!"

"He'll live!"

Bernie was still engrossed with the thought of that lovely naked body on the deep-piled rug in front of the huge open fireplace at his mother's house. Now would be a good time, he thought, his mum was shopping and not expected home until well after dinner as she was to visit her sister at Surrey Hills. Shit of a place to live that was, Bernie had spent a school holiday at Aunt Bea's place once - that was enough. Doris cut in to his thoughts.

"Hey! It's getting cold, what's doing?"

Hell, there was an opening, thought Bernie and he jumped at it.

"Let's go to my place, get the fire going and you can play me some records. After dinner we'll take in a movie, should be a hot sexy one on somewhere!"

"Suits me!"

She rose and was in time to witness the ambulance whip around to where the fight had taken place.

"Hope he's all right, Bernie!"

"Yeah!"

They walked as it was only around the corner to their destination. Their lovemaking began as soon as the front door closed behind them. Bernie was whispering in her ear and kissing her neck as they entered the lounge room and even before the fire was lit, they were on the settee getting heated. They fell to the floor and Doris eased him away.

"Don't spoil it! Get the fire going and I'll have a shower ready for us."

"Mmpf."

Bernie kept kissing her shoulders and neck as he massaged her tight little breasts.

"Bernie!" She almost growled.

"Huh? Yeah, sure - sure, in a minute."

Doris rolled away.

"Now Bernie, or you'll waste it!"

"Okay, okay!"

He scrambled to his feet and Doris saw he was truly excited. She wondered if his zipper would stand the strain. It did not take Bernie very long to have a roaring fire warming the room. He closed the doors so the room would heat up more quickly, placed a record on the player - making sure it was a long playing full-sized LP and poked his head into the shower. Doris, naked, dragged him in - clothes and all.

"Hell woman, wait cantcha?"

He struggled out, stripping quickly and shaking the droplets off before they could soak in properly; then hung the clothes to dry on the towel rack. They had a fun few minutes before Bernie led his dripping prize to the lounge room, unmindful of the water trail left behind but taking towels to dry themselves in front of the comforting glare of the fire. A passionate love-session got under way as they embraced and manoeuvred on the lush mat before the steady warmth. Bernie had well and truly struck home when a key clicked the front door open and his mum yelled out.

"Are you there Bernard, I'm home!"

"Shit!" Bernie whispered, not missing a stroke, then louder - "I'm in here Mum - with Doris. Don't come in yet!"

"Oh!"

She stopped, and then repeated.

"Oh! Er - I'll go in the kitchen and put the kettle on."

She could be heard busily preparing the tea. The lovemaking continued until they were sated. The fire beamed its approval in witness of the happy couple at peace.

"Hi Mum!"

A happy Bernie greeted the plump rosy-cheeked woman who was stirring vigorously at a pot on the stove. She did not look but sensed the two people there and could imagine her boy's arm around the waist of the red-faced Doris. It was a scene that she had witnessed before.

"You might have saved me the embarrassment, Bernard, there are times and places you know!"

His mother glanced at Doris.

"Hello Doris."

The girl went a shade redder as she replied.

"We're sorry Missus Luntz but --"

Bernie cut in.

"Expected you would be at Aunt Bea's Ma, you said you were going there!"

"She wasn't home. Did you leave the room tidy?"

Missus Luntz poured three cups of tea as she was answered.

"Yeah, the bathroom's a mess though; I'll clean it after dinner!"

He pulled a chair across for Doris, and then seated himself.

"Needn't bother, I'll do it myself, it will be done properly then."

Missus Luntz sat herself down and they quietly sipped tea. She spoke absently.

"Bit of a commotion down the street, your mate Billy Dramford was rushed to hospital. Some people say he's dead!"

"Christ!"

Bernie jumped up, knocking his chair over and raced to the telephone. He frantically rang the hospital. His Mother's shocked face received only a sad shake of the head from

Doris, who remained silent. There was considerable urgent conversation from Bernie as he spoke over the 'phone in the lounge room. Eventually he replaced the receiver and returned to the table.

"Well, what was that all about?" His mother demanded.

"He's all right – I said I was his brother – slight concussion and a broken nose, that's all!" His relief was obvious.

"Oh, I'm glad Bernie!" Doris put her hand on his.

"Concussion – broken nose – and you are glad. For God's sake what is going on?"

Bernie's mum was indignant.

"We fought over Doris, I knocked him down, and that's all!"

"I told you not to take Karate lessons, one day you'll kill someone. Looks like you damn near did now!"

"Dammit all Mum, I didn't use Karate. It was good old straight boxing like Dad taught me. I beat him and he tried to kick, I grabbed his leg and he hit his head on the ground; that's all there was to it!"

"I still say fighting is a brute bully way to settle a difference. You got a bloody tongue in your head, why don't you use it 'stead of carrying on like a flamin' larrikin!"

She was hostile, her eyes blazing as she went on.

"It's the twentieth century now; you are not living in the dark ages of Gladiators!"

Plates were set and piled high in silence. An uneasy lull hung over the table as they ate.

"I'm not going to apologise, Mum. It could have been me in that hospital, if Sharkey had his way."

Bernie suddenly blurted. It had taken a little while to say, as he had been brooding over his mother's words. She kept her peace and said nothing. The meal was dispatched in silence.

Bernie rose and pecked his mother on the cheek.

"Thanks for the dinner Mum; Doris and I are taking in a movie. We won't be home until late, so don't wait up for us. Cheerio!"

Missus Luntz shook her head, sighed and then began clearing the dishes. As Bernie hurried Doris across the road, he was thinking of how close he must have come to killing Sharkey. He had always hated the little shit and their fight was inevitable. Bernie was extremely jealous when Sharkey had begun to try and steal a march with Doris but somehow he thought Doris would be above Sharkey and not succumb to his amorous advances. But, Sharkey sure had a way with the girls and after all, Doris was a warm-blooded human. Also Bernie realised, he had never actually proposed to her or anything, they just accepted the fact of keeping company. Neither claimed ownership of the other, but Bernie felt slighted when Sharkey just moved in and tried to squeeze him out. Then it came to a head when Bernie was walking Doris to the store for a packet of smokes. Sharkey moved in and tried to take over – elbowing Bernie out of the way. There was nothing else for it – it was a stand-off, whoever gave way was the loser; both knew it and so did Doris. Who she preferred of the two Bernie didn't know, had Sharkey won she probably would have gone off with him; same as she did with Bernie. It was do or die! The first theatre they passed had a science-fiction movie about 'War Lords of Space'. They gave it a miss and tried 'The Flea-house' around in the main Civic Square. That looked better 'The Sex Siren'.

"Let's try this one, Bernie!" Doris urged.

"Why not?" He answered, delving into a pocket for his wallet.

A shot rang out from a passing car which sped off. Bernie spun around with a gasp, a hand on his shoulder where blood was oozing out. Doris screamed as Bernie slumped to the ground.

Part Two

Lawry Dramford was the eldest child in a large family of rough-n-tumble tough, beer-swilling, smoking, swearing larrikins. There were no other words to explain them. Old man Dramford used to do the circuit of the country towns with a travelling circus. He was a fighter of some small renown on his own dung-heap yet never had the finesse to make the big-time. He did hold the crown in the side-show boxing ring though. Anyone who wanted to bet five dollars they could floor him in two two minute rounds would collect fifty dollars off his manager. To old man Dramford's credit, no one ever did, even if he had to resort to a knee to aid his cause; he sure would. Sharkey took after his old man in that respect and being the baby of the family, it often stood him in good stead against his bigger, tougher brothers. Even so, the blood tie held them together somewhat, birds of a feather if you will. Lawry Dramford could mix it with the best of them but felt he was a bit more refined; he fancied himself as the thinker of the family. To this end, he called on his little brother in hospital. He would get the guts of the matter first then kill the bastard responsible. Sharkey was not pretty to look at, at any time. Now however, what could be seen past the bandages seemed only to be bruises and swelling, distorting his unpleasant features noticeably. He favoured his elder brother with a twisted grin.

"Glad ya come, Lawry!"

"Yeah! How're you feelin'?" Was the dry reply.

"Shithouse, the prick grabbed me foot and slammed me head inta the groun'!"

"Who was it?" Lawry nonchalantly drawled. Sharkey's eyes blazed.

"Luntz - that bloody Bernie Luntz, I'll kill the bastard when I get out!"

Lawry nodded as if it was the answer he expected, and then smartly walked out as he replied.

"No need - I'll get him for you!"

So it was that as Bernie and Doris turned to enter the theatre, Lawry hurried forwards to accost them, fuming because he had not been in time to catch up with them in the darkness by the alley. As the shot rang out and he saw Bernie fall, he quickly ran to the road to see the make and number of the car. In the darkness he could not make out the number but he was sure he would recognise the soft-top Ford Galaxy with flames painted on the rear guards. He was visibly shaking as he joined the throng about the fallen victim. Bernie was sitting against the ticket box in obvious pain, but conscious. Doris was fussing about with his handkerchief, trying to stem the flow of blood from the hole in his shoulder. The bullet missed the bone high on the right arm, it had entered from the back and came out at the front leaving an ugly gaping hole. As he looked past Doris at the milling circle of faces jostling for a look, he saw the features of a Dramford.

"You!" He accused. "Trying to even the score for your brother, jeez, I'll get you for this!"

The surprise on Lawry's face was genuine.

"But I didn't - it come from a car - I don't even have a gun!"

Bernie glared a disbelieving sneer upon his pain-wracked face.

"I'll get you!" He gritted through clenched teeth.

The ambulance came as he wobbled to his feet, holding the bloodied handkerchief to his wound. The Police came and dispersed the crowd, taking statements from all who offered. Lawry Dramford had vanished after the accusation. Bernie stayed overnight at the same hospital as that to which Sharkey had been admitted. It was feared re-action may set in and there was no doubt in the minds of the police that whoever had tried to kill him, would try again. For the life of him, Bernie could not make out what was going on. True, the Dramford's were a mangy lot but he did not really think they would go so far as to attempt to kill, just as revenge for a punch-up. Yet he did see Lawry Dramford on the spot immediately after and he knew Sharkey was still in hospital. The annoying part was that most of the eye-witnesses - and there were many - affirmed what Lawry had said; the shot came from a passing car. If it were true, who and why? Why Bernie Luntz? He did not have that sort of enemies; it did not add up, there was no rhyme or reason for it. Bernie was released and two days later he and Doris were at his home, sipping tea, when a knock sounded at the door.

"I'll get it, Ma!" Bernie said as he adjusted his sling and mumbled. "Why can't they use the buzzer, what do they think its there for?"

As he opened the door, he was surprised to find the caller was Lawry Dramford.

"What the hell do you want?" He snarled. Lawry looked up with pain-filled eyes and gasped.

"Not me - ugh - Bernie. Dark Ford Galaxy - ugh - soft - soft top, flames - I, I didn't - !"

What he didn't, Bernie never knew, because Lawry fell on his face in the doorway - dead; a red pool across his back.

Part Three

Lieutenant Borno of Homicide was not satisfied and again drummed home his query by slamming a fist into his hand. "But why - dammit, why?" He argued with himself. "If Dramford did shoot you, why would he come crawling back here and die on your doorstep. He certainly had no gun and we have searched all of the gardens in the neighbourhood about the theatre and your house. Not a sign of a weapon - I think you are barking up a gum tree Luntz! You would have been a prime suspect after your threats at the theatre but you have an airtight alibi. You have not been alone in two days and you were at home with two witnesses all morning when Dramford came to your door. You say he tried to get you to revenge his brother; yet he crawls to your doorstep with his dying breath to deny it. This is deeper than a bloody fist fight - it's gotta be!"

He sat by the table, drumming his fingers in thought. Suddenly he arose.

"Right, there is nothing more we can do here, we have your statements - just see you stay indoors for a while - until we sort this thing out. Come on Jack!"

He led his assistant to the door, nodding to Missus Luntz and Doris as they left. The bullet hole in Bernie's shoulder was just a flesh wound; it was clean and no doubt would leave a scar. Even though the arm was stiff and sore, it did not hamper Bernie's movements much; so long as he kept his arm in a sling and did not move it about. It was late afternoon when Doris and Bernie - ignoring the detective's order - paid a visit to the hospital to see Sharkey. The heavy bandages were removed from about his head but his nose was still in plaster and a huge patch was on the shaven part at the back of his head. A large gap in his mouth attested the fact he had lost some teeth too. He snarled and looked belligerently at the couple as they neared his bed.

"Well, whatcha want, come to gloat?"

Bernie saw Doris into the visitor's chair then sat on the bed before replying.

"No Sharkey. Look, we came to say we're sorry about Lawry, and want to find out something."

Sharkey sneered.

"That shits me that does, you didn't give a bugger about Lawry. You hated his guts, same as you do mine. Don't tell me you're sorry!"

"All right, so I didn't like him but I didn't want him killed, even if I did think he tried to kill me!"

Bernie's gaze was level as he looked Sharkey fair in the bruised eye. Sharkey dropped his stare and belligerent attitude.

"Okay! What do you want to find out?"

Bernie sensed he was getting somewhere. The sudden loss of his elder brother had taken some of the fight out of Sharkey; he seemed more mellow and reasonable. Bernie asked.

"Did Lawrey have any friends who drive a dark Ford Galaxy with a soft top?"

He watched Sharkey closely but the younger brother really did not seem to know of such a vehicle.

"What do you know about flames then? Last thing your brother said to me was 'flames', what would he mean by that?"

Sharkey frowned as best he could under the sticking plaster across his forehead.

"Damned if I know, he never used to light fires!"

They sat in silence for a while, and then Bernie rose and walked to the window, absently mumbling. "It must mean something - hell - a dying man would not say it unless it meant something. Think Sharkey, I'm trying to find

13

out who killed your brother and tried to kill me; so think damn you!"

Sharkey just shook his head.

Once again they fell silent, and then suddenly Sharkey yelled.

"Grass!"

Both Doris and Bernie looked their amazement.

"Grass I tell you!"

Sharkey spat the words out through the gap in his face.

"Lawry got mixed up with a crew from Bondi; they used to get hep on weed. I remember they came 'round in a battered old Ford one day and Lawry had a dust-up with them over 'grass'. I remember the heap had flames painted on the back 'guards!"

"Could be!" Bernie became interested.

"Names?"

"Jiggered if I ever heard 'em - no, wait - one was called 'Smithy'; Lawry told me he floored 'Smithy'!"

"That's a lead anyhow; I'll get Lieutenant Borno on to it!"

Bernie took Doris by the hand and they made to leave.

"Bernie!" Sharkey halted them at the door.

"Yeah?"

"Lawry was only gonna punch ya as he caught up, the slug that got you mighta been meant for him!"

Bernie thought a moment before replying.

"Yeah, could be. See ya Sharkey." They went to the Police Station.

The next day the police located the car and it was owned by one Terrence Smith, better known as 'Smithy'. It was expected that one of the many eye witnesses should be able to clinch a conviction when the trial was held. The bullet in the theatre ticket box matched the one taken from Lawry's body. Back at the Luntz residence, Missus Luntz had just replaced the receiver.

"I rang Beatrice, she is home. You two will have to get your own dinner, I'm off."

Doris looked at Bernie, raising an eyebrow.

"Okay." He said. "I'll light the fire. You put the record on and get the shower going!"

THE END.

This story contains :-
Gutter language
Swearing
References to Sex and Drugs.

This story is entirely fictitious and any reference to persons alive or deceased, is not intended. This work always remains the express property of the author :-

This story can only be reproduced with the written authority of the author or his agent :-
Rory Curran.

Exit The 'Cross'
by
HOWARD REEDE-PELLING

This story is based around a prostitute and her three associates of the street, who are caught up in the sordid activities of their kind; in the vicinity of 'Kings Cross'. How they aspire to a better way of life and leave the 'rat race' behind them is the essence of this story.

Warning: These works contain:-
Sexual references
Gutter language
Violence
Reference to Drugs.

Howard Reede-Pelling.

This story was initiated on the 7-12-2001 and finished on the 24-12-2001.

Exit the Cross   By Howard Reede-Pelling

Greta sighed as she traipsed jauntily along the brightly lighted streets of the 'Cross'. King's Cross, the hub of activity for night life in a bygone era, had now declined into decadence. Oh sure! The gaudy neon lights still flashed out their messages to attract the tourist dollar; however, the thriving throngs of years ago had dramatically declined. Gone the heady days of rich night life, sparkling limousines and smartly clad business and society couples - no - gone indeed! Sordid little street urchins, pimps, dealers and thuggery, were now the essence of present day fact. The couples slinking through the streets now-a-days were for the most part, same sex couples bedecked with ear-rings, which, more often than not; had nothing to do with ears. Noses, eyebrows and occasionally lips or a tongue, were the recipients of these icons of the decadent society and the depths of despair to which the people of Sydney and indeed, most cities of the modern world; had descended. Sex, crime and violence, was now the norm to which sad and sorry peoples had let themselves become. Law and order became ever more a 'rod' for 'big brother' and 'quality of life', decency and morality had faded almost into oblivion. It was through this scenario that the young, vivacious and curvy tart of the streets, made her pronounced, jaunty and scantily clad way; along the avenue through which she knew a 'customer' would more likely be found, with the confidence of her kind, in order to obtain the precious dollars that enabled a body to survive. Greta shortened her gait just a trifle so that the stilted walk, caused her pronounced breasts to wobble a little more titillatingly. Her ruse had the desired affect, as she knew it would, for a nice new and expensive limousine, cruised silently to a stop where she could easily converse with the well-dressed, and no doubt, quite wealthy driver. Greta quickly stepped inside as the near-side door opened to admit her; she disappeared within, to be speedily whisked off as the vehicle hastened away to diminish in the murky distance. Two teenage street urchins, who also sold their bodies for the reward of filthy lucre, were well aware of the activities of their female counterpart. They grinned to each other as they bemoaned the fact that it was Greta and not they, who was away with the chance of a huge reward for a night's work.

"Ah! She always was a lucky little bitch!" Spud groaned.

"Yair! Pity it weren't one a' us!" Gerry agreed.

"Or bofe! Ay that would'a been awright - ay? Reckon he was loaded an' could afford us bofe?"

Spud snarled.

"Arrgh! Wot's it matter? She's got 'im an' we ain't. Let's git along to the park an' see who's about!"

Gerry obediently followed as Spud led the way. Meanwhile, as the limo' cruised hastily away, Greta eyed her prospect with the measured judgement of her kind. Her practised eye led her to believe that the weedy little fart in the

expensive 'Italian cut' suit would be 'easy pickings'. Maybe she could lift his 'roll'. A wry smile curled her lower lip as the kilometres passed.

Soon the vehicle came to a stop outside a motel on the outskirts of the city. Greta's victim eagerly whispered "won't be a sec" as he hurried to reception. Shortly, he returned with a key and they stopped once more; this time, outside the unit in which he hoped to satisfy his sexual needs. Greta had quit the vehicle and patiently waited as her 'client' opened the unit to her. They entered the sparsely furnished room.

"What's your name honey?" He asked, and then when she told him, he added.

"I'm Terrence - wanna share a shower?"

Greta shrugged.

"Whatever turns you on - it's your dough!"

Terrence smiled as he began to disrobe. Greta too, began to undress, slowly taking off her cashmere pullover.

"Race you in!"

He smiled eagerly as he disappeared within the shower cubicle and adjusted the water flow to a comfortable temperature. So soon as Terrence entered the shower area, Greta had deftly picked the man's pockets, taking his wallet and car keys. She carried her pullover and left the room; closing the door quietly behind her. By the time Terrence heard his limousine roar into life and had raced from the shower to investigate; Greta had flown the coop! Spud and Gerry were sprawled out beneath the shady out-flung limbs of a huge Moreton bay fig tree, in a popular area of the Domain Gardens; when they saw that same expensive limousine in which Greta had departed with her 'prospect'. The two street kids were amazed to see Greta was driving it and she was alone! They were not surprised to witness her park the vehicle by the gardens in that remote spot and abandon it. She hurried to the seclusion of a well protected park bench, which was surrounded by dense shrubbery. The youths quickly made their way to the same area, making sure that Greta was unaware of their presence. Stealthily creeping nearer, the boys eagerly peeped from their cover to witness the prostitute rummage through her ill-gotten gains.

"Phew!"

Greta gasped, as she counted the large denomination notes that were extracted.

"Over a thousand dollars - lucky little me!"

"Yair! An' lucky little us - ay?"

Spud broke from their cover with Gerry hot on his heels.

"Yair! Lucky li'l us!" he echoed.

"Piss off, you pair of Fairies; this's MY earnings!"

Greta snarled as she stuffed the loot down into her cleavage. The wayward young lady quickly rifled through the papers in the wallet, before flinging it into the bushes, some credit cards following the money into her cleavage. She attempted to go her way, but Spud intervened.

"We saw ya git th' prick an' we saw ya come back wiv 'is car. We know ya did a 'job' on 'im - give us a bit an' we saw nuffin' - come on Greta - ya got plenty!"

"Stuff off! I done the job - I get the pickin's!" Greta glared at them. Then,

"Oh! Alright - but you saw nothing - okay?"

She threw a couple of fifty dollar notes to the ground. The youths sprang for them.

"Ripper Greta - thanks!"

They went their separate ways, satisfied.

Chapter Two

'Tearing' Terry Trabert was a muscle-bound oaf of quite limited intelligence, however he did have the courage of a cornered rat and the street-wise credibility of one calling; albeit that of a 'pimp'; or dealer in human suffering. Tearing Terry got his nick-name because of his lack of tact and the fact of an habitual saying, 'o'l tear yer 'ead orf'! He claimed as his own, many of the back streets of 'The Cross', in Sydney. A continual verbal and sometimes physical war, was ever to be witnessed raging in those areas, whenever he had to dispute this claim with the other claimants of the said territory. Often vicious knife and sometimes, gun battles, were the result of territorial bickering. That Greta had 'scored' without his aid came to Tearing Terry's notice through the grapevine and because her 'pickup' was from his territory, then he demanded his cut. To this end, word was passed about that Greta should contact 'Tearing', and pay her dues. That 'Tearing' had no part in attaining the 'customer' was merely a formality. It was his territory, Greta was one of his' girlies' and that is all there was to be said about it - Greta must give her earnings to Tearing and he would allow her a percentage. The girls had no time or a great deal of respect for Tearing, but they were fearful of his violent tantrums, temper and those bulging muscles; which he was not averse to using on the more vulnerable 'weaker sex'! Although fearful, Greta was not one to be taken lightly; even from a bully such as 'Tearing Terry'. She had won her gains without him and they were rightfully hers - nothing at all to do with Tearing. This time Greta would fight for her rights. It would be a boon to her self-esteem if she could win out against 'Tearing', and show the other people he used, that they would not take any more shit from him. After all, the muscled lout rarely did bring up many 'customers' for the girls and then took the greater share of the earnings for himself. This was going to stop if Greta could do anything about it;

she must. 'Tearing' was being a drag on their lifestyle, making them work for peanuts. Greta had to get assistance; she could not do it alone. To whom could she turn for aid? The other girls were all being bullied and although they too, were trying to rid themselves of this muscle-bound millstone, they knew that they were no match for him. Broken facial bones or perhaps a slashed cheek is what they would suffer for turning against the bully. Greta's mind reverted to the two 'Street Kids'. No! They were too juvenile and nowhere near a match in physical strength, against the more mature and violent 'Tearing Terry'! Greta began to doubt her ability to defy her 'pimp'. Perhaps it was just a pipe-dream she was indulging in - a fantasy!

Spud and Gerry were being 'Sussed up' by a prospect. He was rather rangy looking, in that he was quite tall, slim and had an awkward gait as if at some time or other, perhaps the result of an accident; his legs may have been damaged. The man was in his mid-thirties and had a wicked gleam in his eyes, which nervously darted hither and yon - the youths imagined this affliction was drug related.

"Ay - you - the li'l prick; ow much ya want?" He ignored Spud as he spoke.

"'Undred dollars - we share ev'rythin'!"

"Chris', fer that I want yez both!"

"Okay!" Spud agreed. "In the shithouse over there!"

"Hrrrmmph!"

The tall man grunted, and then limped off to disappear within the isolated conveniences. Spud urgently whispered to Gerry.

"Same job! You git down behind 'im an' o'l push, then we bofe jump 'im together - okay?"

"Yair!" Gerry agreed.

When the prospect was bewildered and struggling upon his back on the dirty, wet floor of the toilets block; Spud and Gerry deftly 'lifted' their victim's valuables. Watch, wallet and the surprise and bonus for the pair, was a loaded pistol, stuck in the man's belt by his hip pocket. The youths ran helter-skelter from the scene of their robbery, to disappear in the outer reaches of the park; their victim shouting blue murder and dire reprisals should their paths ever cross again.

Greta and one of her female associates were conversing heatedly in the same quiet secluded area of the Domain Gardens, where she had previously shared some of her 'spoils' with Spud and Gerry. Both were incensed and infuriated at the unfair tactics of 'Tearing' and his ilk. They were at their wits end as to how the larrikin could best be dealt with, and whom, if anybody, they could enlist to aid their cause successfully. It all came to a head in the most dramatic and unexpected manner. The girls saviours too, were from an unexpected quarter. 'Tearing' Terry Trabert burst in upon the two girls suddenly and with fists flying. He had thumped each of the girls with his fists and was standing over their prostrate forms as they lay bleeding from their mouths and sporting swollen features, the while he rebuked them loudly, threatening more of the same - before the young ladies had fully realised what had inadvertently happened.

"Piss off 'Tearin', o'm warnin' ya - an' leave us alone. O'm warnin' ya jus' this once, arse'ole!"

The demand took the pimp by surprise. He glared angrily over his shoulder and beheld Spud, with Gerry slightly behind. Tearing Terry was about to spring at the youths to deal with them, when he caught sight of the gun in Spud's fist. He stopped short, and then sneered.

"You snivelling little dickhead, it prob'ly ain't loaded an' you ain't got the guts!"

Tearing took a step towards the two youths. The gun discharged and a piece of Tearing Terry's left shoe burst, with part of his little toe.

"Shit!"

He screamed as he jumped away, charging through the bushes for cover.

"An' fuckin' stay away from us - we've 'ad ya - arse'ole!" Spud yelled defiantly after him.

"O'm as big as you are now, an' o'm gunna get ya!"

"Shit Spud! Ya showed 'im, dinya?" Gerry exclaimed, in awe. A little of hero-worship showing. Spud quickly moved through the bushes where Tearing had vanished; only to see him limp into his car and with a vicious backwards look, drive off.

"Yair!" Spud gloated. "I ain't gunna stand no more shit from 'im now, neither!"

He assisted the girls to the park seat. They seemed a little shocked by the speedy events.

"You two okay?" He gruffly asked.

Greta's friend, Dolly, replied.

"Yes Spud, and apart from a sore and swollen face - the big shit - I'm okay. Are you alright Greta?"

She turned to see for herself, as Greta nodded. Greta's attention though, was for her saviours.

"Where did you get the 'piece' Spud?" She asked, then, "Thanks - I never thought you had it in you, we better scarp it. The cops'll come you know; let's scoot!"

The four victims of Tearing Terry's past abuses, were walking along one of the side-streets of the 'Cross', chatting excitedly of the morning's adventures. Greta ushered them into a 'Coffee Shoppe' and shouted all refreshments.

Gerry had proudly explained where and how Spud had become the proud owner of a weapon. The girls were quite elated that this had provided Spud with the gumption to stand up to their 'pimp' and Spud, of course, bragged largely that he could now protect them all.

"We'll have to lay low for awhile, to let 'Tearing' Terry cool down a bit!" Dolly mused.

"Yes! And the cops - they'll be on the lookout for us, if anyone actually saw us leaving the spot where the shot was fired!" Greta put in, worry creasing her brow.

"Ah! No one saw nuffin' - I looked!" Gerry answered hopefully.

"Wouldn't like to bet on it!" Spud frowned.

"Everyone who heard the shot would'a looked towards where the shot came from!"

All sat quietly sipping coke or coffee, cogitating.

"Anyway boys, we both want to thank you for helping us - what made you do it?" Dolly asked, then added. "Thought you and Greta weren't friends!"

Spud sheepishly answered.

"Ah, no! We never really been bad friends - 'ave we Greta?" She smiled slightly, shrugging. Spud went on.

"Y'see, she give us some dough yes'ty when we wos really broke an' needin' it - an' we hate 'tearin's' guts any'ow!"

Spud was silent for awhile, thinking, and then spat out.

"Ay! If we four stick t'gether an' look out fer each other - you know - 'elp each other if someone's in trouble, or low on dough - I reckon we'll be better orf an' may get rid a' that big galoot! Whatcha say?"

He looked from one to the other. Greta glanced at her friend Dolly, who raised her eyebrows and pouted; then a slight nod was detected.

"Can't do any harm!" Greta said. "We can give it a go - for a while anyhow - sort of test run, okay?"

All smiled hugely, and settled with a handshake. Three most angry men were in the neighbourhood. Each holding a deep grudge against three of those in the pact of togetherness, the wealthy motorist, the lanky lame druggie and Tearing Terry Trabert. All were separately dreaming up dire reprisals against the rotten mongrels who duped them out of their property and money. Each began their search for recompense and revenge.

Chapter Three

"O'l tear their fuckin' 'eads orf!"

'Tearing' snarled as he puffed repeated small spurts of cigarette smoke from between rotten, stained teeth; the while he glared angrily up and down the alleyway in which he was lounging.

"That bloody snivelling li'l Spud dickhead an' 'is scrawny shit of an 'anger-on, ain't goin' ter get the better a' me - not by a long-shot! O'l tear their ruddy 'eads orf!"

He reiterated.

"Who y' talkin' about?"

The nervous man beside him asked. 'Tearing' Terry grimaced as he spat out.

"Two 'a me hired bums - they bloody-well took a shot at me. O'm gunna git 'em; just you bloody wait. They ain't gunna shoot 'Tearin' Terry an' git away wiv it! Wonder where th' li'l prick got the 'piece?"

"Eh?" The nervous one asked.

"What piece. Was it a Browning Automatic?"

'Tearing' looked fixedly at the questioner, appearing to recall events.

"Stuffed if I know, the li'l beggars ain't never 'ad no 'piece' before!"

He shook his head disbelievingly.

"They 'ad ter of pinched it from somewhere!" 'Tearing' muttered.

"Bastards!" The lanky one exclaimed.

"Who are they? If ya know 'em - bloody tell me - I'll tear their bloody heads off for you; the pricks pinched it off 'a me! Who are they - what's their monikers?"

The nervous lanky man took 'Tearing' by the collar with both hands and pushed him against the wall, the wild eyes darting frantically about. Momentarily 'Tearing' remained against the wall, pinned by his associate and forgetting his superior strength, with the shock of the attack and the apparent instability of his nervous assailant's mental capacity.

"Spud an' Gerry! They's on'y teen-agers, I know where they 'ang out - leggo - we'll git 'em tergether!"

The wild one released his grips and turned away.

"C'mon, show me where!"

It was an order. 'Tearing' obeyed as he realised that between the two of them, he would get his revenge and maybe, 'Lanky Lennie' could shoulder the blame, should things get out of hand. If Spud could be done away with, the little arsehole would then be at his mercy and would come into line. 'Tearing' had a wicked gleam in his eyes as he hurriedly led his hostile associate to the errant pair.

Meanwhile, the wealthy motorist who lost his wallet and credit cards to Greta, at the motel; was cruising the streets near where he had previously 'picked up' that prostitute, named Greta. Having recovered his limousine by asking at the local Police Station, where a council worker had reported the magnificent vehicle abandoned, the man mumbled to himself.

"Strangulation is too good for the brazen little hussy!"

Terrence eagerly scanned the faces of the passing parade strolling along the streets. He momentarily parked outside a cafe' as he strained his eyes to catch sight of the rotten little thief. He opened his eyes wide and a satisfied smirk crossed his face, as two young ladies and two youths emerged from the cafe', right there in front of him. One of the ladies was Greta; he smiled grimly. Quietly alighting from his limo', Terrence quickly walked up behind the four as they wandered away from the cafe'; in eager conversation. He grabbed Greta very firmly by one wrist and applied a 'hammerlock'; viciously twisting the young prostitute's arm up behind her back. Greta shrieked in pain and alarm as Terrence dragged her to his waiting car, the door of which he had left open. Bustling her in past the driver's seat, he hastily shut the door as he settled in behind the wheel and switched the ignition on; the engine

29

purred into action. Greta's three companions, taken aback by the sudden eruption of violence, momentarily stood stunned; taking in just what was eventuating. When Spud recognised the limousine he immediately realised Greta's danger and hastened to her rescue. Terrence had the driving side window open and Spud's pistol pressing against his cheek, as he slipped the vehicle into drive gear.

"Turn 'er off or I'll blow yer 'ead orf!" Spud grimly ordered. A swift upwards sweep of his right arm brushed the pistol away from his face as Terrence applied the accelerator. With spinning wheels screeching upon the bitumen, the powerful limo' sped off; leaving Spud with a bruised wrist and causing the pistol to discharge as it fell into the driver's lap! The bullet left a hole in the roof of the vehicle just above the seal of the windscreen. Greta screamed in panic. Dolly and Gerry ran to Spud's aid as he nursed a bruised arm while standing on the roadway. 'Tearing' and the wild-eyed 'Lanky' Lennie came racing up to them. Surprised, Spud just managed to duck as 'Tearing's' huge fist whistled over his shoulder. Spud sprang away, only to be collared by Lennie.

"E's mine!" Lennie snarled, shaking the hapless Spud unmercifully.

"Where's me 'piece' arse'ole? Gimme it 'fore I smash ya rotten little 'ead on the footpath!" Lennie firmly held Spud by the collar the while he 'frisked' the shaken youth. 'Tearing' sprang at Spud once more, murder in his heart. Dolly and Gerry jumped between the two thugs and their smaller associate.

"Wait!" Dolly yelled urgently. "I know where the gun is - we'll help you get the gun back - just leave Spud alone and I'll tell you; okay?"

"Listen you slut! I got business wiv all 'a you lot, an' I don;t give a stuff about the 'piece'; o'm gunna murder yez all!" Tearing snarled.

Lennie put Spud behind him to halt 'Tearing's' mad lust for revenge momentarily.

"Hang on - you can fix 'em up later - I want my 'piece' first. Just 'ang on a minute!"

He glared wildly at Dolly.

"Where is it? Tell me or I'll break 'is rotten li'l neck!"

Terrence had grabbed the fallen pistol and aimed it at Greta, as they sped ever away towards the motel of their previous encounter. He was aware that Greta knew he had it, by the frightened looks she gave towards the weapon.

"Just sit nice and quiet 'til we get there, Honey." He cautioned. "Then we can settle our differences and maybe you will be good enough to return my wallet and credit cards, eh?"

His severe look bode ill for the terrified 'street-girl'. She just nodded. Greta was at her victim's mercy and knew by the fact that he had hunted her down and taken her that he was indeed a very dangerous adversary; not to be taken lightly. Once inside the suite at the motel, Terrence waved Greta towards the double bed, with the gun; then slipped the weapon into his trousers pocket.

"Give your handbag to me!" He demanded.

Greta tossed it to the end of the bed near where Terrence was standing. He emptied the contents onto the bed. He took all of the money available, which only amounted to seventy-five dollars; his credit cards were slipped into his shirt pocket with the cash.

"Where's all the dough and the rest of the credit cards?" He quietly asked.

"Tossed the others away with the wallet!" Greta surlily answered.

"What about all the dough?" He urged.

"Stashed in a safe place an' you don't get it if you hurt me!" Greta sneered.

The slitted eyes of her captor blazed momentarily; then softened as he forced a grin, as of a fox stalking its game.

"Tell you what!" Terrence stated suggestively. "You give me a good time tonight and we'll split the rest of the cash fifty-fifty, eh?"

"Honest?" Greta queried, wide eyed.

She did not for a moment believe the businessman, expecting that he was softening her up just so he could recover his money; then after using her, he would probably bash her and take his revenge for her previous 'job' on him.

"Sure Honey!" He purred. "I'll treat you really good and maybe we can become regular friends - what do you say to that?"

Greta shrugged.

"S'pose so!"

Terrence went to the door of the unit, turned the key to lock it, and then placed the key in his trousers pocket with the pistol.

"Okay Honey!" He purred, in an oily voice.

"Let's strip off and get this show on the road; and this time - no funny business - okay?"

He dis-robed, taking the trousers with the key and gun and also his shirt with the pocketful of cash; into the shower-room with him. Greta eyed the man's clothing as it hung on the towel-rack beside the vanity basin below the mirror. Her mind ever alert for an opportunity to grab and run, as was her wont. Terrence gave the nervous girl little chance to try a repeat performance. He took her gently by the wrist and virtually dragged Greta into the glass-sided shower cubicle. He indulged in petting, caressing, fondling and gentle kissing upon her neck, breasts and lips. Greta did no resisting and let her 'client' have his way. Eventually, he could hold himself in no longer and suddenly emerged from the shower to dry. Terrence threw a towel to the dripping girl and went to the bed, taking his clothes with him. He threw them on to the bedside chair and guarded them, the while he gloated over the naked body of his prize.

"Come girl, before I lose it!" He ordered peremptorily.

Greta obeyed and the two engaged themselves. He, enjoying himself immensely; she, dormant and lifeless as a rag doll. Her mind racing in urgent haste to overcome the dilemma of staying out of harm's way - for she knew that Terrence would not honour his offer of splitting the money stolen from him - and when it was recovered; Greta had no doubt at all that he would exact some form of revenge for the trouble she had caused him. The act of sex itself had little impact on Greta; it was her calling; her way of life, a means to an end. When they were dressed, Terrence surprised Greta by suggesting they should go to the Motel dining room for a meal - he would pay! The light food and a bottle of wine had Greta soften her fears of the rich man who bought her favours. His light repartee during this unexpected dinner had Greta actually giggling and in fact, quite enjoying herself. He, on the other hand, having sated his sexual appetite and indulged in food and drink in the company of a quite good-looking female, although a bit street-worn, began to thaw in his aggressive attitude towards her. Greta came to relax and feel more composed. When they were replete, Terrence brought the 'street-girl' back to earth by announcing.

"Right, time to go fetch the rest of my money - let's go girl!"

Chapter Four

Dolly managed to pacify Lanky Lennie with the threat of him losing his 'piece' altogether, if any harm befell the two youths or her. The mere fact of Lennie's unstable mental condition due to his drug habit had 'Tearing' go along quietly with Lennie's wishes. His chances with his 'stable' would eventuate after Lanky got his weapon back.

"Alright Girlie!" Lennie hissed, his wild eyes dancing excitedly. "Ya promised me 'piece' - where th' shit is it?"

Dolly was frightened at the suddenness of the events of the past few minutes, her heart beating frantically.

"Spud had it but lost it when the bloke who took Greta raced off in his car - it fell into the car!"

"What!" Lanky Lennie sprang at Dolly.

"You bitch! You said you could get me 'piece', you lyin' little - !!"

Dolly jumped back out of the angry man's way.

"No! I only said I knew where it was - but we can get it - calm down bugger you, calm down!"

Lennie stopped, glaring wildly.

"'Ow" He demanded.

"Spud!" Dolly answered. "Spud knows the limo' and it will be easy to identify because there was a shot fired. It will have a bullet hole in it somewhere!"

Lennie stood stock still, cogitating.

"How we gunna fin' a bloody limo' what's pissed off somewhere in Sydney?"

Eagerly Spud answered.

"I can fin' it - I know where Greta takes her hits. If we get in 'Tearin's' car an' go cruisin', we can track 'er down!"

"Yair!" Gerry echoed. "Spud's good at that; 'e'll find it!"

Lennie looked at 'Tearing'.

"Can 'e?"

Begrudgingly, Tearing Terry nodded.

"Yair! Ain't much th' li'l prick don't know about what's goin' on aroun' abouts 'ere!" Tearing towered over Lennie, belligerently.

"But if ya usin' my bloody car yez are gunna pay f'rit, I ain't no bloody philly - phillyatro - I don't do nuthin' fer nuthin'; it'll cost ya!"

"Awright, th' piece is worth a few bob - o'l pay ya back - now let's git goin'!"

Tearing Terry drove his car to Spuds directions with the wild eyed Lanky Lennie beside him in the front passenger seat. Dolly sat in the back nearside seat beside Gerry, who had Spud at his right. The youth pointed over 'Tearings' shoulder out of the driving side window. "Down that there street - see the motel - that's where she takes 'em!"

A thorough search of the car park and surrounding streets, gave the quintet to understand that the limo' they were seeking, was certainly not at the motel car park or in the near vicinity. Consequently, it fell to sound reasoning that neither was Greta or her 'customer'.

"Ya flung me a bummer, ya li'l prick!" Lennie snarled.

"Ang on - we'll try another place - she's got lotsa 'em!" Spud defended. "Take a right at the intersection 'ere an' 'ead fer the Bull's 'ead 'otel, it ain't far, jus' about - !!"

"Awright - awright! Don't ya think I know all th' pubs aroun' 'ere?" Tearing yelled, cutting the youth off mid sentence.

"I know 'em all I do, guzzled at 'em all I 'ave!"

Two more venues were researched in the quest for Greta and her 'customer', without success; Lennie was becoming highly incensed and quite agitated.

"Right, that's it - pull off th' road here - I'm gunna smash 'is rotten li'l 'ead in!" Lennie growled.

"After me, that was the deal!" Tearing stated, with a snarl. "I'll do 'em all!"

"What about the Highway Motel!" Dolly urged, wide-eyed in panic.

"Greta sometimes goes there - so do I - it's just a few kilometres up this road. It's worth a try!"

Tearing looked at Lennie, with raised eyebrow. The wild one nodded, as their three captives breathed a silent sigh of relief each. Quiet ruled supreme as they motored the little way to this, their final attempt to locate the two who held the answer to the whereabouts of Lennie's 'piece'. Grim faced, the five peered into the car-park of the motel as they entered the surrounding driveway; which circumnavigated the rambling country-style rooming house.

"There it is!" Spud urgently yelled. "That there long black one - see it?"

"You three stay put, an' don't move!" Tearing grimly hissed.

He took the keys from the ignition switch and pocketed them.

"C'mon Lennie - let's git 'em!"

The two ruffians approached the door of the room outside which the limo' was parked. The door was locked. They peered through the window. The suite appeared unoccupied.

"Ain't anyone in?" Tearing stated.

"Yeah, looks like!" Lennie agreed. "We'll try th' dinin' room!"

Once again the two peered through a window. As Terrence and Greta dined, the subject of the little man's missing money was being discussed.

"You promised I'd get half if I take you to it and you won't hurt me - promise?"

Greta pleaded.

"Sure Honey - sure - 'course I will. I promised didn't I?"

Greta knew she could not trust him. She casually looked out of the window, trying to find an answer to her dilemma. How to rid herself of this little leech and still retain his money. Two well-known faces peered back through the window. With a stifled gasp, Greta leaned over so that she would be hidden from view of the window, by Terrence.

"Whatsamatter, you taken ill?" Terrence queried a worried look on his face.

"No! It's my pimp and Lanky Lennie - he's a crazy drug addict. They are looking for someone and I think it's me! We better scoot and quick, they are both very dangerous. How can I get away from them? They will kill me if they catch me!"

She had a genuine look of alarm on her pretty features. Terrence arose and calmly said.

"Come, let us leave!"

He left enough money on the table to pay their way and took his 'lady' by the arm as they walked to the door.

"But they are just out there!"

Greta cringed behind the man as she made the obvious statement.

"They will keep their distance; I have the gun, remember?"

He strode manfully to the door. Tearing and Lanky were about to enter; they both sprang for the couple emerging but stopped short at sight of Lennie's gun pointing at them.

"Ay! That's my piece! Gimme th' bloody thing an' yez c'n go free!" Lanky Lennie declared.

"Bullshit! I want her - O'm gunna strangle th' bitch!" Tearing snarled. "O'l rip 'er bloody 'ead orf!"

As Greta cringed behind Terrence, he smiled grimly and shook his head.

"You are not touching my lady here or I'll put one of these slugs in your guts - no - I'll smash one through your knees. As for the gun, well, when we are leaving the premises in my car - I'll drop it by the gate - I really don't need it. So let us pass or you'll both have to crawl home with broken knees - move!"

Two angry men stepped aside and let the couple pass.

Meanwhile, the three young people in Tearing's car, were discussing their situation.

"Ay! We can piss off now - o'l drive!" Gerry eagerly stated.

"Oh, do you think we should? They'll get us you know, they'll track us down. Anyway - they took the keys!" Dolly worried.

"Shit, we don't need keys, do we Spud?" Gerry asserted.

"Nah!" Spud answered as he ripped the wiring from behind the dashboard.

"There! I've fixed it!"

The engine roared into life as Spud settled into the driver's seat and reversed the vehicle.

"O'm drivin' Gerry - you look too young an' th' pigs'll take after us if they see ya!" Spud stated as he gleefully sped the vehicle out past the reception area. 'Tearing' Terry Trabert and 'Lanky' Lennie were cautiously looking for an opening, by which they could 'jump' the weedy little cock sparrow who was holding them at gun point, with Lennie's stolen gun; when 'Tearing' saw his sedan screeching past with the three young people whom they both thought would stay put, escaping in it with happy smiling features.

"Hey! You arseholes!"

Tearing shouted at them, fists waving frantically.

"O'l rip yez bloody 'eads orf; come back 'ere wiv me car!"

Lennie kept an eagle eye on the gunman and his pistol, as Terrence and Greta made their way to the limousine. They settled inside, Terrence still pointing the dangerous end of the firearm in Lanky Lennie's direction. Terrence quietly drove to the entrance gates of the motel, stopped the limo' as he dropped the pistol beside the main upright on the driver's side, and without a backwards glance, motored away. Greta sat passively, trying to conceive a plan by which she could elude her captor. 'Tearing' raced after his sedan and came to a stop near the gate. He casually walked over to where the pistol was dropped and picked it up, as Lanky hobbled across, shouting.

"Gimme my 'piece'! That's mine!"

'Tearing' handed the weapon over and his associate stuffed the gun into the band of his trousers; by the back pocket.

"Ahhh! Heeled at last - now I feel properly dressed! What do we do now?" 'Tearing' Terry turned a very grim face towards the lanky one and quietly hissed.

"Dunno about you - but I'm gunna tear a little turd's 'ead orf!"

'Lanky' Lennie followed 'Tearing' Terry to the roadway, where they flagged down a taxi and returned to their habitual haunts, on the look-out once again for the two youths and Dolly. Taking Terry's car was the last straw, he swore blue murder that he would rip all their heads off; on the other hand, Lanky was reasonably happy with the recovery of his 'piece'.

Chapter Five

"Well! Which way do I head for - where's our money?"

Terrence casually asked Greta with a smile, as they cruised along the highway back towards the City of Sydney proper. Greta looked incredulously across at the driver, who made this unexpected statement.

"Our money?" She asked.

"Sure, we made a deal and I always make a point of honouring business deals. That's how I became a multi-millionaire. The few dollars you took mean stuff-all to me; it's just the principal of the thing that counts. No one takes me down, I get what's mine and I pay what is owing!"

"Then, you mean I can really keep half?"

Greta asked again, disbelievingly. Terrence pulled the limo' over onto the side of the roadway. He chose a quiet area away from the busy vehicular traffic.

"Got a proposition for you!"

He began. Greta remained silent to hear him out. He continued.

"With all my wealth you are probably wondering why I bothered with a girl like you - eh?"

Greta nodded.

"Had to make a settlement with my missus. She was barren and I wanted a family. We had a few fights over it but my lawyers got me off the hook and now I'm free again. She's been making me go without for a couple of years now, and I'm a red-blooded bloke - I need a woman around who can satisfy my sexual needs. I've been looking for a few months and after today, I think I have found the fiery little bitch I need!"

Greta sat spellbound by this little man's admissions.

"Yes! What's all this leading to?" Her eyes wide in wonderment.

Terrence pouted before replying.

"Want you to come and live with me for a little while. If we manage to get on well together and you don't get too uppity - well - I er, I may make the arrangement a little more stable!"

Terrence looked deeply into Greta's face.

"You know, you really are a quite attractive girl and I'm sure a little make-up, not that over-painted shit you have on now; and a decent wardrobe - I think it will make a real lady out of you - what say Honey! Are you interested?"

Greta was nonplussed. Never in all her life had she ever dreamed of such a proposition. Thoughts of her present life-style and her way of living with it's ups and downs, daily terrors and future uncertainties, the rough and tumble of the slum areas which she had to frequent because of that life-style, and the thought of her bloody-minded and unwanted 'pimp', Tearing Terry Trabert; began to make this unbelievable proposition look quite attractive to her. Greta nodded to herself as she analysed the implications of her consent.

"How are you working my payments? I'll need plenty if I have to buy new clothes!"

"Then you'll do it?" Terrence eagerly asked.

"I'm thinking about it - you - you won't be brutal, will you? I was really scared when you dragged me away from my friends!"

Terrence appeared to mellow.

"No Honey, I was a little rough on you because you took me down; nobody does that to me and gets away with it!"

He placed a hand gently upon Greta's arm - not her upper leg - Greta noticed as he continued.

"Promise I won't be rough and you will be treated like a lady, but there is one proviso - I need you to quit the streets altogether. No one else ever - just me! What say, will we give it a go?"

Greta was beginning to warm to this very opportune proposal. If she was really treated as well as Terrence had promised, this could be a golden opportunity for her to better herself. It was a way to pull herself out of the mire and degradation of her present lifestyle, but what of her friends? Dolly had become a close friend, they had much in common. What would become of her, they relied upon each other's friendship. Friendships were a very strong bond in the neighbourhood in which their lot had found them. Spud and Gerry she could do without. The little faggots could well take care of themselves and they meant nothing to her. But then, she had made a pact with the youths and they did come to her aid at a very auspicious moment; their intervention may have stopped the two girls from a more serious injury - possibly broken bones - or even death! The two thugs, who were after them all, were very unpredictable. Somehow, Greta knew that she should share her good fortune with the two boys. A pact on the streets was binding!

"I'll make a go of it on one condition!"

Greta eyed Terrence as she tentatively asked a concession.

"Spit it out!" He urged.

"I can't leave my best friend on her own, she needs me as a friend and I need her. Is there some way she can live with us too?"

Terrence smiled an oily smile.

"Great! Hope she's a good looker! I have a big enough house - it's a mansion - plenty of rooms for a good house-keeper servant. If she'll do that, she's in - er - does that cover everything?"

Greta nodded and quietly answered.

"Yes!"

Her agreement regarding the two youths would be honoured once she had Terrence well and truly tied to her. She would bide her time to broach the subject regarding them. They may not even want to move into a house anyway and Greta had no idea at present of how on earth they would fit in; time would tell! Spud, Gerry and Dolly were in high spirits, having eluded their over-bearing captors and escaping their vicious clutches in 'Tearing's' sedan.

"We had better not go back to the 'cross' again just yet!" Dolly said, as she applied thick layers of make-up to her once pretty face.

"If Tearing gets his hands on us he'll kill us or - worse - I know the bastard; he'll mutilate me for sure!"

"Yeah!" Spud mused. "'E'll kill us all. 'Specially now we've took 'is car!"

The handsome face of Spud grimaced with a sneer.

"'E ain't gettin' 'is bloody car back neither. O'm gunna use it 'til it runs outa juice, then o'm gunna torch it! I owe the rotten 'ound that 'cos what 'e's done to us an' 'ow 'e's treated us!"

"Ay! Can I do it Spud - can I?" Gerry eagerly asked.

"I 'ave ter git even wiv 'im too - please Spud - lemme do it!"

The keen childish eyes of the junior member of the trio caused Dolly to giggle.

"Go on Spud, do let him, he has earned it!" She begged.

Spud answered begrudgingly, his own features softened a little.

"Yeah, I s'pose!"

"Yippee!" Gerry interposed.

Spud drawled on.

"Really wanted to do it meself, though I owe 'im more than jus' torchin' 'is car!"

Dolly brushed her short locks with the mechanical action of a cat tending it's young.

"We better not get rid of the car just yet Spud!" Dolly noted.

"We can use it to find Greta. She's one of us and we can't leave her to face 'Tearing' on her own, we must find her. I think she will be dropped off near the cafe' where the rich guy picked her up; let's cruise around there and get her to come with us!"

Spud nodded.

"Yeah! S'pose we'd better - we'll need dough - an' she'll be loaded now, I reckon!"

He glanced at the petrol gauge.

"'Ow much you got Dolly? We 'ave ter git some petrol or we ain't gunna go far!"

Dolly rummaged in her bag, opened her purse and extracted a twenty dollar note.

"Here, take this and you do the driving 'til we get to the Service Station. You better let me drive then 'cause I have a licence and you don't. We have to be careful not to be caught by the pigs in a stolen car!"

"Arrghh! She'll be sweet, I look older'n I am an' 'Tearin'' ain't gunna report 'is car stolen. 'E don't want no pigs askin' 'im questions!"

"Just the same, until we get Greta back - I will drive around 'The Cross'. After, when we head out, it's all yours - you and Gerry can do what you like with it. It's my money paying for the petrol!"

Dolly was determined, knowing it was the safest way to do things.

"Dolly's right Spud; you know 'ow much we been picked up!"

Gerry made up Spud's mind for him. If the junior thought that way, it must be obvious.

"Yeah! Awright!" He consented.

Gerry leaned over to take the steering wheel off Spud.

"Ay! Let's 'ave a drive. I ain't 'ad a go since that Commodore we knocked off las' week!"

"Piss off Gerry, I'm doin' th' drivin'!"

Spud jostled the cadet away.

"Don't cause trouble Gerry. After we get Greta and we're safe somewhere, Spud'll let you have a go then!"

"Yeah!" From Spud.

The tank topped up and with Dolly driving, the three happy young folk enjoyed a leisurely cruise in and around King's Cross, in Sydney. The first pass of the cafe' they were all wont to frequent, was fruitless, in that no sign of Greta or the big black limo'; was to be witnessed. Dolly drove through some of the other areas in which she and Greta plied their trade. Again making a pass of the cafe', Gerry moaned.

"Ah! We're wastin' time; she ain't 'ere!"

Of a sudden, a musical horn was sounded. Spud turned to the sound, jeering.

"Ah shaddup! Wot else did ya get fer Chris'mus?"

"It's the limo' - Greta's limo' - she's in it!"

Gerry excitedly shouted. He was right. Dolly parked 'Tearing' Terry's sedan and the limo' pulled over and parked behind. Greta was out of the limo' in a frantic dash to greet her best friend. They fondly hugged each other. The two youths hovered in the background awaiting the outcome of the meeting.

Dolly and Greta approached Spud and Gerry as they lounged against their stolen sedan.

"Wot's 'appenin'?"

Spud asked as he ran his fingers through stringy fair hair; his mother's pride and joy when he was but a youngster. Life upon the streets away from regular grooming and lack of suitable conveniences, had taken their toll.

"Listen boys"- Dolly began with a huge smile -

"Greta's got something big going with this rich client of hers and they want me to be in on it!"

She stressed the next point by placing a hand upon each boy's shoulder.

"Remember our pact; you know how we're going to look out for each other?"

They nodded expectantly.

"Well, this is the big one; it may get us all out. Just be patient and give me and Greta a week or so - understand?" Dolly seemed dazed.

Something WAS going on and the two youths looked their bewilderment. Greta came across.

"Spud, Gerry, look - I er - Dolly and me have this big chance here of getting out of 'The Cross'. We can't take you yet but we will. Just give us a week to set things up!"

She passed over two hundred dollars.

"Take this an' don't go near the old haunts again, 'case 'Tearing' or Lanky gets ya - piss off somewhere - where can you go that I'll find you again?"

"Me uncle's - you know 'im 'e 'ad ya once out to th' farm; we can stay there fer a week wiv this dough! E'll do anythin' fer a few dollars!"

That settled all then departed as it was quite risky to linger needlessly where Tearing would come across them.

Chapter Six

Lanky Lennie and Tearing Terry split up to go their various ways, after the taxi-cab had gone. Lennie had his 'piece' back and although still out of pocket and in need of revenge against the two youths; he knew that sooner or later their paths would cross again and then would be time enough to exact his revenge. 'Tearing' on the other hand, had been embarrassingly short-sheeted and not only did not get monetary satisfaction, but possibly lost his means of transport to boot. In theory, steam was escaping from his nostrils and his terrible temper began to affect his whole being.

"Bastards! Rotten bloody bastards!"

He exploded as he viciously kicked a plastic garbage bag that was awaiting collection near the gutter side. As the bag flew through the air it broke asunder, spilling the putrid contents all over the roadway.

"An' that's only half a' what'll happen to 'em when I get me mits on 'em - geez - I'll tear their bloody smart-arse 'eads orf I will!"

'Tearing' Terry Trabert entered the first 'pub' he came to. It would be very remiss of the man to actually pass a hotel. He sat alone guzzling 'grog' (his usual pastime) and dreaming up dire revenge upon the two 'street-kids', whom he claimed as part of his 'stable' of prostitutes; along with Greta and Dolly.

"They ain't goin' to make a fool outa me, can't 'ave the rest a' me girls gettin' uppity; it ain't good fer me image!" He mused to himself.

"I 'ave ter make a example of 'em - or o'l 'ave a rebellion - none a' 'em will give me a cut!"

Tearing Terry kept drinking until he could no longer think rationally. He arose, drunkenly shouting.

"O'l tear their 'eads orf. Tha's what o'm gunna do - tear their bloody 'eads orf!"

The drunken lout staggered his way outside, expecting to find his sedan where he usually left it. The vehicle was nowhere to be seen. Slowly reality dawned; his male prostitutes had flogged it!

"Bashtards!"

Tearing screamed as he sank down against the wall of the pub, to the footpath, where he fell asleep.

Spud and Gerry found it hard to explain their good fortune as they drove away in the stolen vehicle. They not only had a car and the freedom they always enjoyed with one, but the two hundred dollars freely given to them by Greta.

"Ya think we orta do what Greta says?" Gerry asked of Spud.

His senior cogitated momentarily.

"Nah! I ain't afraid of Tearin', 'e don't scare me; I took 'is car didn't I?"

"Yeah! We ain't afraid 'a no one, are we?" The youngster echoed.

"Although". Spud drawled, thinking deeply.

"Greta may be right ya know!"

"Wotcha mean?" Gerry queried, wide eyed.

"That rich 'hit' a' hers. She reckons 'e's loaded an' she' reckons as 'ow she's gonna share some a' it wiv us. 'Member, she's got sumpin' big goin' wiv 'im, an' we can be in on it - week or so - she said.

Sub-consciously Spud had directed their joy-ride in the direction of his uncle's farm, some forty kilometres out of the city. It was a real hay-seed of a joint, with only two milking cows and the man supplemented his pension with the annual annuity from the agistment of a few head of hacks. The man was the essence of a hayseed himself.

A weedy little old-timer with long lank shoulder-length hair, which sprawled from beneath a dirty, stained felt hat bedecked with flies. He did not have the sense to soak the sweat out of it and so discourage the pesky little beings. Jarrod Menton lived alone since his wife died after a fall broke her pelvis and pneumonia set in; over a decade ago. His lonely life led him to need Greta's services one time, through the agency of his wayward nephew, Spud. Any visitor was a welcome diversion from his loneliness. The arrival of Spud and Gerry was cause for a huge toothy grin.

"Heh, heh, glad yez come Spud - er - is that young Larry with you?"

"Ya silly ol' coot - 'is name's Gerry!" Spud frowned.

"Ya mem'ry ain't gettin' no better, is it? We're gunna stay a week - okay?"

"Ain't got no tucker. Did yez bring some grub?" Jarrod asked, hopefully.

"Yeah! Stopped at th' General Store jus' down th' road apiece - brung a slab too!"

Spud proudly showed the goodies as he unloaded the sedan. His uncle slapped Spud on the back; most happy at the sight of the life-saving provisions and at the same time, eyeing the beer impatiently.

"Yez always was me fav'rite nephew!" He grovelled.

"Hey unk! O'm yer on'y nephew!"

"Ah! Details, details. Let's git stuck into th' grog!"

The trio entered the rickety old house to indulge in their piss-up!

As Terrence silently cruised his limousine through the automatic gates and along the gravel driveway, his home loomed luxuriously through the surrounding shrubbery of the well-kept gardens. Indeed the home was a mansion! Only two stories high but quite broad, and the rear section seemed to disappear forever amongst the solid garage, storage rooms and caretaker's cottage; which also hid amongst the evergreen foliage that made up the beautiful gardens. Greta and Dolly gasped their amazement.

"Crikey! How many people live here?" Dolly asked.

49

"Only me and an old Chinese cook. He lives in a couple of back rooms that I had put aside especially for him. It's separate from the main house in that I had it sealed off with it's own en-suite and kitchen. There is a connecting door through which he comes to serve my breakfast and sometimes I summon him for supper if I have been working late. Otherwise we leave each other alone. He is too old now to do much and he has served my family well for most of his life; so I have virtually retired him. That's another reason why I could do with a cook-dishwasher. Mostly I dine out!"

Greta made what she thought was an inspirational comment.

"Then how come the gardens are so well-kept?"

"Gardeners come in three times a week. They use the rear gate as I gave them a key. They come and go at will so I don't need to be bothered!" Terrence answered.

When the limo' was suitably garaged, he ushered his two young ladies inside the mansion via the connecting garage door. It led directly into a passageway that had a parlour to the left and the kitchen to the right.

"There's a powder-room directly ahead, when you have freshened up, come into the kitchen; I'll have a cuppa ready!"

The following week saw a huge transformation in both Dolly and Greta. Terrence organised an under-study, to allow him a week away from his office. The week became both a hectic and most enjoyable pastime for all three.

Sauna, Boutique, Beauty Salon and Footwear Emporium, was capped off with a visit to a jeweller; where inexpensive baubles gave a final decorative touch to the two transformed ladies. Terrence beamed his approval as he wined and dined the new residents of his luxurious home. Indeed, the beautification of the pair of 'street girls' by professional people, needed to be seen to be believed. Terrence applauded his own insight and deemed it good judgement. Dolly could well understand Greta being feted and offered a home under the circumstances in which Terrence found himself. She could also see that Greta would jump at such a lift in her life-style and also the fact that she would want to enmesh her best friend in that change-of-life. What Dolly could not comprehend, was that Terrence had taken her in just on Greta's whim; perhaps - no, for sure - the man had ulterior motives. Both young ladies realised that their bodies were the price of this new life-style. Both also knew that the life-style would pay better than the streets in the long run, even if not in monetary reward; certainly in a higher standard of living and a 'peace-of-mind' betterment. That they were readily available at the will of their benefactor, was a way of life with them anyway; so the sexual side of the arrangement had little impact or worry upon the two. As Greta was his chosen lady, she was to share the master bedroom with Terrence. He bowed to her wishes of an adjoining bedroom initially, so that she could more easily acclimatise herself to this sudden burst of opulence; altogether foreign to her. Dolly on the other hand, was more than satisfied with her own rooms, which were handy to the downstairs kitchen; in the housekeeper/maids quarters. After the initial evening out to dinner, the three people sat at the kitchen table of the mansion, discussing the future and what Terrence would be expecting of the ladies. His demands were few, but his stipulation that he would not stand for theft or insubordination, was most profound. Knowledge of his 'ladies' prior habits and way of life, made the man most adamant that nothing of the like nature would be tolerated under his roof. Immediate cessation of their verbal agreement and eviction from his home, would be the aftermath of any such misdemeanour's. The girls promised to abide by these provisos.

'Tearing' Terry Trabert awoke from his drunken stupor in familiar surroundings.
"Shit!"

He roared at the world in general, as he eyed the bars in the cell in which he was incarcerated.

"Them arse'ole bloody pigs got me again!"

'Tearing' rose unsteadily from the floor upon which he was laying and peered through the bars.

"Oy! Lemme out buggar ya; I ain't done nuthin'!"

"Keep it down or you'll stay a week!" A gruff voice boomed.

Footsteps were heard as the guard approached. Having slept off his drunken state, 'Tearing' Terry was allowed to pollute the streets again with his presence. Unable to drive anywhere due to the loss of his sedan, he was forced to walk or take public transport; cabs were too costly. His temper was approaching boiling point and were he able to get his hands on the two young culprits who caused his discomfort, murder may well have been attempted. Sober and needing transport, 'Tearing' Terry enlisted the aid of an associate of the streets. 'Dirty' Henry was a slim but wiry thief in his early thirties. He would acquire anything or any given article for the right price - any price was the right price - Henry was negotiable. Of his few possessions that were legitimate, 'Dirty' boasted a battered old van of the blunt-nosed variety. Ancient though the vehicle was, its reliability made the van a most valuable means of transport.

"The snivellin' 'ounds what took me car is prob'ly pissed orf up th' bush somewheres!" Tearing snarled.

"But o'l find 'em when they git back - geez they's gunna pay - they'll wisht that they didn't cross me; you'll see!"

"Yeah!" Dirty agreed. "You'll fix 'em up proper, you will!"

"Gotta find them sluts, Dolly was wiv 'em but I reckon Greta 'as more idea where th' boys went. O'l bloody shake it outa her; she better cough up or o'l rip 'er bloody 'ead orf!"

Chapter Seven

Although the pair of ruffians toured all of the usual haunts and areas in which 'Tearing's' quarry were in the habit of frequenting, not a sign of any of the four young people could be found.

"Someone must know where th' buggars are!" 'Tearing' growled.

"Ay! There's young 'Curley', ain't he a pal of that Spud prick you're after?"

'Dirty' exclaimed, as he thumbed at the gangling youth who leaned against a wall, puffing on a cigarette. 'Curley' snarled.

"Yeah! Wotcha want?"

As the snub-nosed van pulled up along the gutter where he was stationed.

"Spud! Where's Spud, do ya know Curley?"

'Tearing's eyes blazed fiercely as he demanded.

"Ow th' 'ell would I know? I ain't 'is nurse-maid!" The curly headed one spat out.

"If 'e ain't at the 'Cross', where does 'e 'ang out. You know 'im good as anyone don't ya?" 'Tearing' Terry persisted.

"Might! It'll cost ya!" 'Curley' sneered.

"Five bucks. Take it or o'l rip yer fuckin' 'ead orf!"

'Tearing' offered the cash.

"Try 'is uncle's place out to th' foot a' th' Blue Mountains. 'Member sumpin about Merton's Lane, forty k's along the 'ighway - fink 'e said it was th' second farm on th' right. I know its just after some crummy bridge where they's grouse fishin'!"

Without so much as a 'thank you', 'Dirty' and 'Tearing' departed hurriedly.

"What makes ya think th' boys'll go there?" 'Dirty' asked.

"They ain't game enough t' stick aroun' 'ere now they've crossed me, an' they've took me car. Little buggars always nick orf fer a joy-ride when they nick some wheels. They usually torch 'em too - geez - they better not torch my sedan; o'l rip their bloody 'eads orf!" 'Tearing' stated, worry creasing his forehead.

It was a fruitless search. Although the two had a leisurely drive along the freeway and onto the highway which led to the Blue Mountains, they could not locate Merton's Lane; or any lane for that matter which even faintly resembled it in name. At the forty kilometres mark, there was a roadway but it was no lane. The surface was heavily bituminised and the road was actually a main route between two large country townships; one either side of the highway. Travelling backwards and forwards for over three kilometres both to the left and right of the highway; also proved fruitless. The ruffians were stymied and 'Tearing' Terry became ever more furious as the money he gave 'Dirty' was being eaten away with the cost of fuel.

"We ain't gettin' nowhere!" 'Dirty' growled.

"Yeah! I know!" 'Tearing' acknowledged.

"Better piss off back 'ome an' o'l 'ave a go at that bloody 'Curley' again!"

Back at the mansion, Terrence and the two young ladies, whose fortunes had changed for the better; were enjoying a relaxing day in the small indoor heated pool. It had been idle for many months but with the advent of the two fresh young faces about the house, Terrence deemed it opportune to have the pool cleaned and rejuvenated. That his wisdom was paying off became evident with the joyful banter and caressing touches, his two new house guests shared with him. Li Chan was also enlisted to bring refreshments. Something useful for him to do for his master, made the old man very happy, as he did lead a boring life.

"Terrence Darlin'".

Greta cooed, as she brushed a wisp of wet hair out of her benefactor's eyes.

"Are you happy with Dolly and me so far?"

Her wistful look gave the man to understand that she was after something.

"Oh! And if I am?" He asked, guardedly.

"Oh! Just something that I have been wondering for awhile!"

Greta pouted, and then appeared to change the subject.

"Do we have to call you Terrence? Don't you answer to a more comfy name - what's your nickname - or maybe your mum's pet name for you?"

"Eh? That's not what you started to ask me!"

He sat up to look a little more deeply into her face.

"Yes! I do have a nickname - 'Tiddles' - mum used to call me 'Tiddles'. I always checked the finances at home and mum reckoned I was 'Tiddling' the books, so she landed me with that! Started in my teens and stuck with me for life. Some of my staff still use it. Got to have a little dignity at the top you know.

"Oh! That sounds cute. Could we call you 'Tiddles'?"

Dolly asked her eyes wide and an expectant look on her face. Terrence reddened a little and appeared coy.

"Only in private - 'round the house - okay?"

"Great Tiddles!" They chorused, giggling.

"Now!" Terrence asked. "What were you really going to ask me, Greta?"

She brushed a forefinger down his nose as she whispered.

"The caretaker's cottage, is it ever used?"

"Huh?" His surprise was obvious.

"No - why - what's it matter. Don't tell me you want to move in there?"

Greta gave a sly wink at Dolly, which was not lost on Terrence.

"I - er we - Dolly and me, were just wondering if maybe, you know, a couple of our friends might be able to use it?"

Terrence showed amazement.

"Of all the cheek! You want to turn my home into a bloody brothel? Not a chance!"

His sudden eruption had the girls back-peddling. Dolly put on her charm to try and resurrect what may become an embarrassing incident.

"Ah Tiddles Dear -!" She cooed.

"Not girlies. We wouldn't try that on you; I mean, you have been so sweet to us and we don't want to rock the boat. It's the two boys - they're only kids - you know the two with Greta and me when you snatched her from the cafe'?"

"Hrrmmpf!" Terrence snorted.

"Just a couple of larrikin kids. They'd probably steal my mansion from me and wreck the cottage! What are they to you anyway?"

'At least he was listening', Greta thought, as she put her weight to the argument.

"They have been very sweet to us an' saved us from a real bashin' from 'Tearin'! We made a pact that the four of us'd look out for each other. Dolly and me will keep 'em in order - truly Tiddles - couldn't ya give 'em a chance? Please, we owe 'em you know!"

Terrence shook his head slowly as he mused to himself.

"Gotta stand firm, give in once and before I know it I'll be forced out of my own home!"

Alarm showed in his eyes as Terrence mumbled the cautious warning to himself.

"Tiddles' Dearest, please give the boys a chance. They've been kicked from pillar to post and from joint to joint, an' never had a chance to make something of themselves. We promise they won't be any trouble an' we will keep them in order - Dolly and I will - truly! Please 'Tiddles', pretty please?"

Greta cuddled close as she softly bit her benefactor's ear, then planted a sloppy kiss upon his forehead.

"Oh! Alright - alright. But no trouble, you two keep them out of the mansion - okay? They use the rear gate and stay only at the cottage or they're out on their ears. The first sign of any damage or noisy parties an' such - they get booted out - that's as far as I go. No more after that; I got four people when I only opted for one! Do you understand that? 'Nother thing"- he added - "they keep to themselves and I'm not keeping them in food or clothes!"

"Thanks 'Tiddles' you are a dear!"

Dolly also kissed Terrence upon the forehead, adding.

"We will make sure they behave themselves!"

Although he had many misgivings regarding his 'ladies', Terrence found the remainder of the day to be most pleasant, in that he was feted and doted upon. Greta and Dolly kept him in good humour and really went out of their way to take his thoughts away from the subject of the two youths. The girls did not want Terrence to change his mind.

Jarrod Menton was sozzled! It had been some time since he had an opportunity to 'grog on', as he had been doing through the advent of his nephew's arrival. Over the week his visitors had stayed, more than one slab of beer had been consumed. The fact that Gerry was well under age to drink alcohol did not come into the equation. At seventeen, Spud was able to pass at the local store as an adult more so since he always drove his stolen car there; to pick up supplies. Even though most of the time the three were intoxicated, Spud still had the presence of mind not to 'torch' their only means of transport. Twice he had to foil Gerry and halt his juvenile wilfulness; for the youth was ever one for mischief.

"Ya can torch th' flamin' thing when we are finished wiv it - not b'fore, buggar ya!"

Spud flung at the boy, as he delivered a backhander.

"Ah shit!" Gerry whined.

"It on'y b'longs t' Tearin', so 'oo cares?"

"We do, ya arse'ole. 'Ow we gunna git back t' the 'cross' wivout it?" Spud growled.

"Oh yeah, didn't fink a' that!" Gerry submitted.

It eventuated that the money Greta had obtained from Terrence and gave to the boys; ran out. Spud and Gerry reluctantly left the quite disappointed Jarrod, who requested the boys to return, so soon as possible. On their return to the King's Cross area, Gerry urged Spud to let him drive 'Tearing' Terry's sedan into a quiet cul-de-sac and 'torch' it! Finally the cadet had his way and reaped his revenge upon the bully 'pimp', whom more than once, had flogged the boy for not earning enough or not giving 'Tearing' his share!

"Revenge is sweet, ain't it?"

Gerry grinned, as the pair fled the scene, only to return as a few onlookers gaped at the burning vehicle; so they could relish their handiwork.

"Wot now?" Gerry asked his mentor.

"We gunna fin' someone ta 'roll'?"

Spud elbowed his cadet in the ribs gently.

"Don't haveta - we're goin' lookin' fer 'Lanky'!"

Spud enjoyed the surprised look on Gerry's face as he made the statement.

"Shit! Whaffor? E'll kill us, we took 'is roll an' 'is 'piece' - are ya crackers?"

Gerry stood quite still and his bewildered look caused Spud to chuckle. Smugly, Spud elaborated.

"Sumpin' you don't know. I went through 'Tearin's' car while you was tiddly, an' I found some 'smack'! They's at least four grams an' 'Lanky'll fergit wot we done if 'e gets it cheap!"

"Is it pure?" Gerry asked in awe.

"Nah! Don't fink so. 'Tearin' is on'y a piker, 'e couldn't pay fer th' good shit!" Spud said.

"'Ow much can we git f'rit?" Gerry's eyes were wide and eager.

"Prob'ly worth a couple 'a grand but 'Lanky' won't 'ave that sorta dough either; I reckon 'e'll give us one grand but, an' let us off th' 'ook!"

"Grand's better'n nuthin' ain't it? I reckon we'll fin' 'im at th' park - 'e usually 'angs aroun' th' park!" Gerry asserted.

"Yeah!" Spud confirmed. "Good a place as any ter look."

"Geez! We'll 'ave ter keep a lookout fer 'Tearin' though. 'Im an' 'Lanky' Lennie 'as been aroun' tergether a bit lately!"

The boys found 'Lanky Lennie sitting on the seat by the shrubbery where they shot at 'Tearing' Terry and so rescued the two prostitutes.

"Chris' you arse'oles got guts comin' t' me meek as y' like. I owe ya I do - what's on - did yez come willin' t' get throttled?"

Lennie arose with revenge in his heart and murder in his eyes.

"'Ang on 'Lanky', we come ter pay ya back. Got sumpin' for ya - sumpin' ya need - we'll flog it real cheap t' ya!"

'Lanky' Lennie eyed the two cautiously.

"Yeah! It better be bloody good. Wot ya got?"

Spud dangled the four one gram bags of heroin temptingly in front of the tall addict. His eyes glowed appreciatively.

"Loverly! Is it clean?" He asked, reaching for the plastic bags.

"'Course it is - don't fink I'd get ya rubbish do ya?" Spud queried, cockily.

"'Ow much ya want f'rit?"

"Cos' ya two grand!"

"What? It's probably ain't been 'cut'; give ya five 'undred!"

"Fifteen!" Spud bartered.

"Eight 'undred!"

'Lanky' grabbed at the bags, Spud was quicker, expecting the move.

"Thousand neat an' it's yours!" Spud settled.

"O'l 'ave ter taste it!" 'Lanky' stated.

"Where's th' dough?"

"I don't carry that sorta loot on me - yez'll git it ternight!" Spud nodded.

"Okay, yer git it when we see yer cash an' no fuckin' tricks 'er o'l take it ter th' big guys!"

"O'l be 'ere, I want th' shit" 'Lanky said, eagerly.

Chapter Eight

It was just at dusk that Dolly was driving slowly around the perimeter of the Domain Gardens; one of her old haunts. She was on the lookout for the two youths, when they suddenly burst out through the bushes where she and Greta used to rendezvous. They ran helter-skelter directly towards her. As they tried to by-pass the vehicle she was driving, Dolly sounded the horn and called to them.

"Spud, Gerry, I've been looking for you - hop in!"

Momentarily the boys stopped, bewildered. They did not know the vehicle but recognised Dolly's voice.

"Ay! It's Dolly!" Gerry cried out.

Both youths piled into the car, Spud shouting.

"Fer chris' sake, git goin', an' 'urry will ya?"

As the car sped ever further away from the gardens, Dolly enquired.

"What's the rush - why the great hurry?"

Both Gerry and Spud cast scared glances behind.

"They've stopped chasin' us!" Gerry noted.

"Who - who's chasing you?"

Spud elaborated.

"We wos swingin' a deal wiv 'Lanky' -."

"What! 'Lanky Lennie?" Dolly gasped.

"Yeah! But it wos awright, we wos sellin' 'im some 'smack' wot I foun' in 'Tearin's' car. Trouble wos, 'Lanky' tried t' sell 'alf 'a it t' 'Tearin'' an' they bofe woke t' where I got it. We wos 'urryin' t' git away from 'em - geez it wos lucky you turned up!"

"Ay Dolly, where'd ya git th' wheels - didn't fink you'd flog some wheels!" Gerry asked in awe. Dolly smiled sweetly as she explained.

"I didn't. The car belongs to Greta's benefactor; it was his wife's old one. When they settled up he had to buy her a new car; so now Greta and I can use this one!"

"Great!" Spud interposed. "Where we goin'?"

Dolly broke the news she and Greta were holding.

"Listen up you two. Greta and me have worked very hard on Tid - er - Terrence, that's Greta's client! Now we have a real good thing going with him. We are getting off the streets and we are going to be real ladies!"

"Haw! That's a good one that is!" Spud burst out.

"Shut up you stupid little twit and think!" Dolly scalded.

"We don't want to spend the rest of our lives laying for strangers and getting bashed by 'pimps'! It's our chance to get away from it and lead a decent life!"

Both Gerry and Spud sat open-mouthed. This was a different Dolly to the one they knew. Spud was moved to comment.

"Shit yeah, jus' 'ave a good look Gerry. She's got real duds an' 'er 'air's been done - an' geez - don't she look a spunk?"

"Why, thank you Spud, nice of you to notice!" Dolly appreciated, then -. "Now, if you guys want to get away from 'The Cross', you have a great chance. Greta and I have honoured our pact with you - remember - we worked on Terrence and found you a grouse place to live. There is a catch but - !"

She eyed the two boys carefully as she drove into the driveway of Terrence's mansion.

"Crikey!" Gerry exclaimed in awe.

"Whatcha doin' drivin' in 'ere - ain't we gunna get inta trouble?"

Dolly giggled.

"Dope, this is where Greta and me live, and now you boys can; Terrence said you can use the caretaker's cottage."

"Wow! A cottage a' our own - ya kiddin' ain'tcha?" Spud gasped, disbelievingly.

"No! But there are conditions and you two better behave - alright?"

Dolly urgently asked of them. She drove around to the rear of the premises.

"You two look like real grubs, so just behave properly - if you have any idea how to - anyway; you have to meet Terrence so he can set out the rules!"

"Wot rules?" Spud demanded.

"No pilfering, no fights, no parties and no damage - those rules!"

Dolly gave them a severe look as she laid down the law, the while she led the youths to the back door of the mansion.

"You have to make a good impression!" Her demeanour was harsh and worried.

"Ah shit!" Gerry whined.

"We don't live by rules - we need freedom - let's piss orf Spud!"

Spud became quiet.

"'Ang on Dolly, don't go in yet, we gotta think fings over, I jus' need t' talk ter Gerry a bit!"

"Okay, but be quick about it!"

She waited at the door. Spud took Gerry aside and they had a spirited discussion for a few minutes.

"Righto, o've talked 'im inta listenin' any'ow - let's see the geezer!"

'Tearing' Terry left the local police station in a fuming temper. He had been summoned to be notified that the burned-out remains of his sedan were found nearby. Immediately the 'pimp' knew who to blame, however he said nothing of his suspicions to the police. Instead, he again enlisted the aid of 'Dirty' Henry. Once more the battered old van was needed. Although he knew that the boys were back at 'The Cross'; much searching and numerous enquiries failed to let 'Tearing' know of their whereabouts.

"Geez! They's causin' me some trouble them two is, o'm gunna knock their bloomin' 'eads orf I am!" 'Tearing' snarled to his driver, who responded?

"I reckon! They owes yer a car and they've turned them two girls agin' ya. 'Ow ya gunna find 'em?"

'Tearing' Terry mumbled to himself.

"They ain't anywheres aroun' the 'Cross', so I gotta think where they're at! They'll be shit scared a' runnin' inta me or 'Lanky', so I wouldn't be s'prised if they nicked orf back up t' Spud's uncle's joint again! We 'aveta fin' 'em - let's look for 'Curley' - 'e might 'a 'membered somethin'!"

"Yair! And ya got t' git 'em for trying to flog y' 'smack'!" 'Dirty' added.

"Yeah! Th' rotten li'l mongrels. I 'ad a real job tryin' t' claim it back off a' 'Lanky'. Lucky 'e snatched it outa Spud's 'ands!' 'Tearing' Terry growled.

Finding 'Curley' proved almost as difficult for them as it was to locate Spud and Gerry. He was not in the area where they spoke to him previously and many of the known haunts of his ilk, also proved fruitless. It was more luck than good judgement that caused the two roughnecks to come across the gangling youth. He jumped off the back of a passing truck where he had hitched a ride. They caught up with him as he tried to enter an all-night disco. 'Curley' was about to snarl an angry 'Piss off', when Terry grabbed his arm, but upon recognising the muscle-bound bully; 'Curley' wisely thought better of it. Instead he asked.

"Yeah! Whatcha want?"

"We couldn't find Spud's uncle!" 'Tearing' stated, threateningly.

"Ain't my fault!" 'Curley' replied with almost a whine.

"Ya give us a bum steer, cost me heaps jus' motorin' aroun' an' I paid yez plenty fer nuthin'!"

"Ya prob'ly went th' wrong way!" 'Curley' fenced.

"Gimme it again an' I ain't payin' no more. Ya better git it right or o'l take it outa ya hide! Where's th' bloody farm?"

'Tearing' hovered threateningly.

"Awright, awright. Take it easy!" 'Curley' worried.

"Ya go up t' th' Blue Mountains forty four k's along th' 'ighway, then down Merton's Lane. 'Is 'ouse is jus' past th' bridge - !"

63

"Ya bloody lanky young dick'ead!" 'Tearing' roared.

"Yez tol' me it was forty k's afore - now it's forty-four - make up yer bloody mind!"

'Curley' looked aghast.

"No I didn't, I tol' ya forty four!"

"Arse'ole!" 'Tearing snarled as he clipped the youth about the right ear.

"Lucky I don't rip yer 'ead orf!"

Four kilometres past the main connecting road which crossed the highway, Terry and Henry came across Merton's Lane.

"Bloody shit of a kid!" 'Tearing' swore.

"Why di'n 'e tell us right th' first time?"

"Ah! It don't matter!" 'Dirty' exclaimed.

"We found it, now all we gotta do is locate th' farm. Secon' 'ouse to th' right an' it's jus' past a rickety old bridge!"

"Here's th' bridge comin' up now!" 'Tearing' noted.

"Yeah, looks like, an' there's an 'ouse over there up on th' ridge - mus' be it - wot's 'is moniker?"

"Stuffed if I know - anyway - 'oo cares?"

As the rattle-trap van approached the rickety old home of Jarrod Menton, he stepped out onto the meagre verandah to welcome his unknown visitors. When they alighted and walked towards him, Jarrod asked hopefully.

"Did yez bring any grog?"

Completely ignoring the old man's question, 'Tearing' demanded.

"D'ya know a teenager named Spud?"

The old man brightened.

"'Course I do - he's me nephew - did ya bring him up with ya?"

Jarrod peered past the two men at the van.

"No, we thought he might be up here with you. We need t' talk to 'im, d'yez know where th' li'l bast- brat is?"

Disappointed, Jarrod shook his head.

"Nah! 'E stayed 'ere a week wiv 'is mate Larry no - wasn't Larry; I think it was Terry!"

"Gerry, ya stupid old coot. 'Is mate's name is Gerry. Tell us where they've went or we'll knock ya bloody 'ouse down - we gotta find 'im!"

Terrence frowned deeply and for a moment looked down his nose in disgust at the sight of Spud and Gerry, when they were ushered into his presence, by Dolly. Greta and Terrence were enjoying a coffee in the kitchen, when the trio entered. Greta introduced the boys as she poured three more cups of coffee and issued them around.

"Yeah, gidday!" Spud drawled, as Gerry just nodded.

Terrence waved the boys to a chair each and the five sat about the table, tentatively eyeing each other. Terrence began the conversation with an acknowledgement.

"Yes, I recall these lads now; you -" he pointed a slim finger at Spud - "tried to shoot me and put a hole in my limousine! And now you have the audacity to expect me to put you up; a man would be a bloody idiot!"

The Lord of the manor was becoming heated. Greta tried to placate her benefactor and excuse the youth's actions.

"'Tiddles' - he was only looking after my interests - Spud was trying to rescue me from a kidnapper; remember Dear? He wouldn't have shot you.

The gun fired when you drove off, you nearly broke his arm. Spud wasn't trying to shoot you - that's the pact we made - the one I told you about!"

"Anyone who goes waving guns about is a gangster and too big a risk to let roam about my home -"

Terrence began, but Greta cut him short.

"Careful 'Tiddles', you may have to leave your own home. I can remember someone else who waved that same gun around when we left the motel! Er - is he a gangster too?"

Terrence sat dumbfounded.

"Touché!"

He smiled.

"Suppose you have something there!"

He turned his attention to the waiting youths.

"Greta and Dolly asked me to put you two up - against my better judgement mind - but if I do let you use my cottage; can you guarantee you will behave, be quiet and don't wreck anything?"

He gave the boys a severe look, and then continued.

"I won't have any vandalism or fires in the place. You look like the type of reckless bloody kids who don't give a damn about someone else's property. I know I'm taking a huge risk letting you in, but Greta and Dolly promised they'd make sure you two behaved!"

"Yeah, awright, we won't do nuffin' like breakin' stuff er torchin' nuffin'. We promise, don't we Gerry!" Spud asserted a slimy grin on his features. Gerry acquiesced in the affirmative.

"Wot do we call ya?" Spud asked.

"Mister Primble; I am Mister Primble to you lads. Primble of Primble and Associates. If you can look after the cottage - I may even pay you to do it - perhaps a few renovations if you are willing!"

"Ah! We don't know nuffin' about reno - renova's - wot ya said, we on'y need a bit a' dough fer grub an' a coke; tha's all. We'll git by if we on'y use th' joint fer sleepin' - ay Gerry?"

Terrence took all four of his guests on a guided tour of his cottage.

"Strewth!" Spud exclaimed. "Look at all the old furniture, shit, it mus' be worf heaps!"

"Yes, my word it is!" Terrence proudly affirmed. "You may use it, but do any damage or try to sell it off and I'll have the law onto you in a flash! I'm doing you a favour and being good

66

to you, just because Greta and Dolly asked me to; so don't abuse their trust in you. Do the right thing by me and I can help you get off the streets and lead a decent life. Greta and Dolly can see the sense in it, so get your act in order and take advantage of this golden opportunity being offered to you!"

The cottage was a most comfortable home. It comprised of three bedrooms, one of which was at the front of the house with a living room opposite, in which collectables adorned the walls. A single passageway that led to a lounge room upon one side, and a bathroom upon the other, which led to smaller bedrooms - presumably the children's rooms, was to be locked off. The two front rooms had the majority of the quality furniture and Terrence deemed it appropriate that they be denied the rough youths; at least a small bit of insurance against unwanted damage. The boys were quite happy as they had no use for that part of the cottage anyway. The kitchen, bathroom and two bedrooms were more than ample for their sparse needs, after roughing it in the likes of toilet blocks, sheds and dis-used factories or derelict houses. That they too, had to make use of the back entrance to the cottage and the grounds of the manor, suited them admirably. Terrence gave them the youths the two keys they would need, then he and his 'ladies' retired for the night.

Chapter Nine

Terrence Primble, of Primble and Associates, had found it necessary to attend his business affairs, since in his absence important decisions began to crop up and his presence was required. Greta and Dolly were commissioned to take the youths to a Men's Wear Emporium, with instructions to outfit them in more appropriate attire befitting the elegance of the urban area in which they would now be residing.

"Strewth, new duds!" Gerry exclaimed in awe. "An' we don't 'afta pay f'rem!"

"Geez!" Spud expostulated, a huge grin on his face.

"You ain't never paid fer nuthin', ya usually nick 'em!"

"Yeah I did!" Gerry defended. "I paid fer that 'hit' a 'smack' wot we sold t' ya mate 'Curley', di'n I?"

Spud laughed.

"Ya didn't pay f'rit outa your dough, it was on'y your half a' th' 'hit' we made on that skinny geezer we 'rolled' in th' gardens!"

"Yeah, but it was my dough!"

Resplendent in new clothing, the four were indulging in drinks using the facilities of a nearby café. It adjoined the Emporium where Terrence had allowed Greta to use his credit cards to purchase the boy's clothing; on the assurance that they would not abuse his trust in them. The ladies sat sedately and more or less demurely at the street side tables; out of character with the life they were used to leading and entirely at odds with the lounging sprawl of their younger companions.

"Don't you two feel better now you got new clobber?" Dolly asked.

"I reckon!" Spud agreed, and then sneered.

"Shit! 'E must be nuts lettin' us take 'im fer cloves an' a bloody 'ouse - we got a chance t' make a fortune outa this git!"

His eyes were alight with the fervour of the mischief-maker. Dollar signs were echoed in his brightened, scheming eyes. Greta snarled a timely warning.

"Listen you little shits! We only got you in because of our pact. You helped us so we helped you. Dolly and me won't stand for no stuffing about. This ain't one of your 'hits' - Terrence is my customer and you'll just bloody leave us alone. You stuff about with this chance and you bugger it up for all of us!"

She blazed fiery-tempered eyes deeply into the faces of her underlings. The heat of passion was not lost on the two youths.

"Awright, awright!" Spud agreed.

A panel-van suddenly screeched to a stop on the road opposite the cafe'. All turned to witness the event. None of the four knew the man at the wheel, but all recognised the hated face of 'Tearing' Terry, in the passenger seat.

"Ay! That's Dirty's old heap - 'Tearin' used ter borry it - an' shit! E's in it. We better scoot!" Spud shouted, immediately heading for the driving side of Greta's loaned sedan.

"Piss off Spud - I'm driving!"

Greta pushed the youth to the rear-side door as she scrambled for the keys and set the car in motion. 'Tearing' Terry was halfway across the road, held up by traffic, when the four raced away in the small sedan. Using side streets, and taking a round-a-bout route home, the four young people eluded 'Tearing' and 'Dirty', to safely arrive at their new home; Terrence Primble's mansion with the caretaker's cottage. It was within the cottage and around the kitchen table, that the four were discussing the advent of their former 'pimp'.

"We gotta do sumpin' about th' big lug!" Spud frowned.

"We ain't gunna have no peace 'til we git 'im orf our backs!"

"Yeah!" Gerry echoed. "But 'ow we gunna do that? Ay! Le's git th' boss t' hire a 'hit' man an' do away wiv 'im!" The boy suggested, eagerly.

"Don't be a duffer Gerry!" Dolly chided.

"Fancy expecting a big businessman like Terrence to do that!"

"Just the same Gerry, you may have something there!" Greta said, pouting slightly.

All looked to her in amazement.

"Wot ya mean?" Gerry asked. "I didn' really mean we'd bump 'im orf!"

"Yeah! Whaddya mean?" Spud queried.

Greta elaborated.

"I think if we tell Terrence about him - although he's already met 'Tearing'- he just may come up with an answer to help us. Terrence don't want no toughs like 'Tearing' following us back here. 'Tiddles' has too much to risk losing!"

"Tiddles'?" Spud questioned.

"Terrence - that other's just a nick-name Dolly and me call him - don't you two call him that; he'll kill us!"

"Okay, so how d'ya fink 'e can 'elp us?" Spud pushed.

"Dunno - he's a good thinker but - an' I'm sure he'll come up with something!"

That evening in the comfort of his bedroom and after his sexual needs were satisfied, Terrence became aware of the little extra niceties heaped upon him, by Greta. Being a very astute businessman, it was not in his nature to let the matter of the extra attentions slip; Terrence needed to examine the root cause of them and to this end, he gently questioned his most ardent partner. Her fears of her former 'pimp' were well founded, as Terrence himself had witnessed. He was most sympathetic and gave Greta a good hearing. She outlined in detail the problems that she, Dolly and the boys, faced daily. Greta stressed the fact that sooner or later the big bully or cohorts he may instigate, would come, after following one of the four to his mansion and perhaps destroy or steal. That their safety was heavily at risk became apparent to Terrence. He assured Greta that he would solve their problems provided that she, Dolly and the youths kept their parts in the arrangements and did the right thing by him. Greta promised their overwhelming loyalty to him and reiterated their urgency of wanting to do right by Terrence.

'Tearing' Terry Trabert and 'Lanky' Lennie were indulging in a heated debate with 'Dirty' Henry over the merits and price of a quantity of heroin. All were unaware of the two huge men who approached them as they squabbled in the midst of the shrubbery, where Greta and Dolly usually met to divide their 'spoils'. 'Tearing' was very big and muscle-bound, 'Lanky', tall and wiry but both men were dwarfed by these two newcomers.

"Shit!" 'Lanky' gasped, as he became aware of their presence.

"What do ya want?" His companions jumped nervously, thinking it was a drug-related raid.

"You!" One of the newcomers accused, as he pointed to 'Tearing'.

"You are known as 'Tearing' Terry, and you -" he pushed Lennie heavily to the ground - "are 'Lanky' Lennie!"

"Hey arse'ole - wot's it to ya?"

Lennie screeched as he tried to rise, only to be met with a hearty kick to the ribs. 'Tearing' bored in with heavy fists flying as he snarled.

"O'l rip yez bloody 'eads orf!"

'Dirty' Henry beat a very hasty retreat, leaving his associates to bear the brunt of the onslaught while he protected his 'smack'; not to mention his own personal safety. 'Tearing' Terry and 'Lanky' Lennie were no match whatsoever to the professional 'Bouncer's' who were engaged by Terrence to put the bullies in their places. As Greta's former 'pimp' and his companion in crime, lay swollen, bleeding and broken in the dusty grass area surrounded by shrubbery; they were given their rights.

"You will leave a couple of your former 'girlies', named Greta and Dolly entirely alone. You will also not bother two of your former 'bum-boys', names of Spud and Gerry - do you understand?"

Both Lennie and 'Tearing' glared defiantly back at the 'bouncers' from their uncomfortable positions on the ground.

"Do you both understand?"

The elder of the two demanded, the while he aimed a pistol at 'Tearing' Terry's face.

"Awright! I 'ear ya - 'oo 'ired ya?" Terry fearfully asked.

"Mind your own bloody business. We are well-informed and the first time you dis-obey my orders, you will both be wearing concrete boots! Have we made ourselves clear? Leave the four alone, because if we get called - next time - you've had it!"

Greta, Dolly and the youths were again in the cottage kitchen discussing their situations. Greta was pressing her point with urgency.

"Will you two just wake up to yourselves? Terrence has bent over backwards for us. Dolly and me have never had it so good and it'll get even better. You just don't know how lucky you are - 'Tearing' and 'Lanky' off our backs - they've been bashed and threatened with worse if they bother any of us again. If you boys can just behave, I'm sure 'Tiddles' will look after ya well an' you've got a decent home for life maybe. Jus' don't take him down - don't bite the hand that feeds ya!"

"Yeah! Reckon yer right Greta. Wot about it Gerry - we got a nice place t' doss an' if we 'elp aroun' a bit, we might even git t' 'ave a feed fer nuthin' - eh Greta?" Spud mellowed.

"S'pose!" Gerry reluctantly admitted. "We can allus git our kicks outside somewhere's, an' we's free t' git t' th' Domain if we wanta!"

"Now you're usin' your melon!" Dolly put in.

"We all got a very good reason to better ourselves now - this is the end of the rainbow for us all - are we agreed?"

"Yeah! I can see ya right. Gerry an' me is gunna stick tergether wiv you two, like we done when we made th' pact. Good ol' 'Tiddles'!" Spud exclaimed.

"Mister Primble to you two!" Greta admonished.

"Oh yeah! Mister Primble - good ol' Mister Primble!"

Outside the kitchen door, Terrence grinned to himself just before he knocked for entry.

THE END.

Pat - Tricia

This story is entirely fictional and no reference to people alive or deceased is intended.

Rory Curran.

PAT - TRISHA

At eight years of age Pat was overawed by this, her very first flight. The window of the jet was just too high for her to see out, unless she stood on the seat. Of course the Air Hostess was very kind but firm - children must not stand upon seats that people in nice clean clothes have to sit on - but a couple of rugs folded did the trick well and Pat could then see out. There was not much to see, the jet kept going through fogs all the time. Very soon the rugs were taken and Pat was strapped into her seat-belt. The jet was about to land. The flight from Tasmania did not take long and the pretty lady holding Pat's hand as they made their way along the huge corridor, checked the tag pinned to the little girls cardigan.

"Your name is Lawrence is it - Patricia Lawrence?"

Pat nodded, her lovely dark hair flashing beneath the overhead lights.

"And your Aunt's name is Pamela?" The hostess continued.

Again Pat nodded. The hostess left the child sitting in a conspicuous area and bid her stay put, saying.

"I just have to get your bag from the rack, I will be back very soon. Don't you dare move, will you?"

Again Pat answered with a shake of the head. It was only two minutes later that the hostess returned to find a shapely foreign woman in her early twenties, talking to the little girl.

"Are you Pamela Lawrence?" The Air Hostess asked as she put the bag down.

"Si. Eet is pronounce Low-ren-za!"

"Oh. That sounds French!"

"No, eet is Italiano. This Trisha - her momma and-a papa - such a- one bad thing it a-happen. I got it one bambino I'm a-no want. What I'm-a gonna do with it? Momma mia!"

She threw her hands up in despair, then grabbed the case and led the girl away.

"Lowrenza? The hostess frowned.

"Those accents, what a funny way to pronounce Lawrence!"

As the taxi carried Camellia Lorenza and little Pat Lawrence away to the sleazy back street of an inner Melbourne suburb, Camellia was still mumbling to herself and the frightened little girl.

"What I'm a-gonna to do with you - how I'm a-gonna work. Why you momma do this to me? You just-a one big damn nuisance, I'm-a no want you!"

Pat began to sob softly. She received a severe shaking.

"You don't-a cry! I'm-a no put up with you to cry. You listen at me?" Camellia threatened.

Patricia subsided into a corner muffling her sobs, a most unhappy and frightened little girl.

"You-a hear me Trisha?" Camellia shook her again.

"My name is Patricia, mummy calls me Pat!"

"You don't talk it back at me. I'm-a know you name, don't you theenk my sister she tell it to me? You name its a-Trisha!"

They eventually alighted at a small weatherboard house painted in garish colours. A weedy little man opened the door, a cigarette dangling from his thin lips.

"That her? Pretty little thing - how about gettin' some grub - I'm starvin'."

Camallia brushed him aside, dragging Pat behind.

"You always a-bloody hongry, why you don't open it one tin you useless a-bastard? Get it the bag and pay the man!"

Camellia flung the child onto a dilapidated old couch.

"You want to go toilet, it's-a out there!"

She pointed to the open door. Pat was too frightened to move. She just sat.

It did not take Camellia long to have some hot tinned food on the table. The weedy man opened a couple of cans of beer and they all sat down to the meagre meal.

"Tony, give it Trisha a drink water!" Camellia ordered.

"What the hell good is water to a kid? She needs milk.

"So we don't got some milk do it, you want I give it her one tit?"

"Hey. How'd you like some beer?" Tony suggested. He poured a little into a glass and pushed it towards the child. Pat tucked her chin tightly into her chest and looked away.

"Eat it you dinner." Camellia growled, pushing the plate closer.

Pat took up the fork and timidly picked.

"What we goin' to do with the kid tonight. You givin' up the beat?" Tony asked.

"No, I'm-a work. You do nottink, you stay." Camellia flashed her large eyes in anger.

"Bull, I got a game goin' with Antonio."

Camellia jumped up, pointing a knife at Tony.

"You got it no game tonight. You-a mind my Angela's bambino or I cut-a you dirty neck, you listen at me?"

Tony banged his fist on the table as young Pat hurried from it and cuddled into the old couch, again sobbing.

"Now look what you've done." He snarled. "You frightened th' kid!"

He went over and sat beside her.

"It's all right Kitten, we don't mean it, and we always talk loud. Come on, sit up here."

Tony lifted Pat onto his knee and put an arm around her so that she would not fall.

"Settle down Sweetie, things'll be okay."

Tony then addressed Camellia.

"You know, I think I will give the game a miss tonight. She is a cute little thing, ain't she?" Camellia "Hmmpfed."

78

Part Two

At the time when the Air Hostess was delivering her charge to Camellia Lorenza, David and Pamela Lawrence were riding the Airport elevator and arrived in the lounge seconds after the others had departed.

"Oh David, I am so happy. At last we will have a baby!" Pamela squeezed her husband's arm.

"She is no baby Dear, Patricia is eight. More likely be a damn little nuisance under our feet." David smiled.

"Ah! You know she won't, how long have we yearned to have a child? I know you can't help being sterile and we have tried all the adoption agencies. I didn't think I would ever be glad your sister Jenny was an unmarried mother, but oh. I am so happy she can't manage and sent Pat to us for awhile!"

They reached the area pre-arranged by letter and eagerly looked about for an Air Hostess with a dark-haired little eight-year-old girl. The Lawrence's had no idea what she looked like as the girls mother could not afford the luxury of photographs, however they were sure they would know the little girl by the written description.

"Oh!" Gasped Pamela, rushing forwards. "There she is!"

Sure enough, an air hostess was bringing a small girl with dark curly hair towards them.

"Patricia Dear!" Pamela knelt down to the girl.

"I am your Aunt Pamela and this is Uncle David. Oh you are a lovely little girl!"

Pamela held her hands out to the child but the girl, with hands on hips, stamped a foot peremptorily.

"I am called Trisha!"

"Oh?" Pamela was flabbergasted. "Well now, in the letter I received it is written as Pat. Never mind, it is the same thing. We will call you Trisha Dear. Aren't you glad to see your Aunt and Uncle?"

The arms were still outspread and the youngster stepped into the warm embrace.

"My word" Pamela sighed "we are all going to be so happy together. Come, what say we all go home?"

David carried the child's small case and clasping a tiny hand each, they bid adieu to the hostess and made their way to the car park.

"We had better take the ticket off her now Dear" Pamela suggested.

David unpinned the name-tag from the girl's twin-suit.

"That's funny" he mused, studying it "they have 'Lowrenza' written here; probably misunderstood when writing the ticket."

David shrugged it off as a mistake and put the tag into his pocket. Trisha was quite at home with her aunt and uncle although a little shy and quiet. David and Pamela knew she would soon 'thaw out' and before long would accept them as her family. They were motoring along the Tullamarine Freeway, when Pamela asked.

"How is mummy Dear, is she well?"

Silence greeted the remark and Pamela's smiling enquiry vanished when she looked at Trisha's face. A great frown was upon it and tears were welling.

"Oh Darling!" She cried. "What is the matter is something wrong with Mummy?"

Trisha burst into uncontrollable tears. David pulled into the emergency lane and stopped.

"What is this all about?" He demanded.

"It's all right David, I - I think she has suddenly realised she is miles away from mother and home. Drive on, I will fix it!" Pamela waved him on.

David set the car in motion and hurried home. Pamela unharnessed Trisha and sat the girl on her lap cuddling the little one close.

"What is it dear, what is wrong with mummy? I think you are home-sick!"

Between heaving sobs the girl grizzled.

"Mummy's dead and Daddy too!"

Trisha broke into a fresh outburst.

"Come now Trisha Dear, who put that awful story into your head? Mummy only just wrote me a letter. Someone has been telling you dreadful stories."

Pamela looked at her husband, he just shrugged. What on earth the girl was talking about he could only guess at. Her father was unknown.

"Who told you that?" Pamela urged.

"A lady policeman, she took me away from school and I had to stay with her until another lady took me to a orferage where there were lots of other little girls!"

Again David and Pamela exchanged glances. They let it be for the time being, no sense in upsetting the youngster too much in her new environment. They would investigate more fully when the child was properly settled. Trisha was very quiet as she was shown each room of the new house in which she was to live. Her own room was very neat with pretty curtains and quietly toned wallpaper dotted here and there with pictures of dolls and teddy bears. There was a huge toy bear upon the bed. They led her to it. Finger in mouth, she was too shy to touch it and looked from one to the other.

"Go on" Uncle David urged "it is for you, your little playmate!"

Pamela pushed the bear forwards. Trisha tenderly took it, studied it very minutely all over, and then crushed the bear close to her as she looked up.

"It is the most beautiful bear, can I keep it?"

"Of course Dear" Pamela assured "Teddy will live here at home with us and we will all be very happy. Now I think we had better wash and make ourselves neat for dinner."

She led the way to the bathroom, David contentedly bringing up the rear, puffing happily upon his pipe. His family was now complete.

Part Three

Camellia had gone, she would be walking the streets until well after midnight. Occasionally she could be expected back if the streets were quiet but that usually depended upon the weather. There was no hint of rain about; in fact it was a rather balmy summer evening. Tony did not expect her until twelve-thirty or one. It was possible she may be away all night. Patricia was sitting upon the couch, shivering with uncertainty and was becoming drowsy. Tony decided to light the big open fire in the lounge room. It was unnecessary but would look cheerful and he would enjoy a beer sitting there with the little girl for company. Ten minutes later he had a friendly looking fire crackling and young Pat was sitting watching the flames. Tony never had much time for kids; most of his time was spent in the pub or with Camellia if she had a lousy night. She had been having good nights lately and Tony recalled he had not seen a great deal of her in recent weeks, he was missing out. His idle gaze on the youngster at his feet put a thought into his mind. He grinned. 'Wonder what Camellia was going to do with this little brat, probably teach her to go on the beat. The kid was a bit young yet, still a couple of years and they soon develop.' The beer was beginning to take effect; the child looked a bit blurry.

"Trisha girl, come here Love!"

Pat obediently came. After all, the man was the only one of the two carers who showed a little friendliness.

"Sit on me knee Love, you're gettin' blurred over there."

Pat moved close and Tony lifted her on to his knee.

"That's better. Now if you want you can go to sleep there, can'tcha?"

The girl was too tired to argue; she just leaned back and continued gazing at the fire. Tony rested his hand on her leg.

"Know what? I think it is bedtime for you, we better put your nightshirt on!"

Tony stood the girl in front of the fire and wobbled to his knees. He was just about to disrobe the innocent little girl, when a loud knocking sounded at the door. "Bastard!" He exclaimed and stumbled along the passageway. It was his friend Antonio. He too, had been drinking.

"Hey Tony. Why you didn't come 'round. What's-a-matter? We got a game to play!"

Tony bowed low, almost falling over.

"Come in to th' kindergarten an' help me sit on the baby. No, thas not right, I - I got to min' th' kid!"

"What you talk, what kid?"

"B'longs to Camellia's sister. She died in a car smash an' her husban' too!"

As the two tipsy men entered the lounge they beheld the girl asleep in front of the fire. Antonio peered deeply at her, saying.

"Seems a nice kid."

He put a cushion under her head then covered her with a rug from one of the chairs. Tony looked on owlishly, too befuddled to comprehend the child's needs; if at all he had any idea what they would be. As Tony was too much under the influence of drink to play their game, Antonio decided to sit it out with Tony and joined him in drink. Time elapsed, the men having drunk enough and in the heat of the fire, they dozed off. It was eleven o'clock when the front door clicked open and Camellia ushered a customer into the front room. She left him undressing as she checked the house. All was quiet; she left them as they were and returned to the bedroom. They were fully engaged when the door creaked open and Pat demanded.

"I want to go to bed!"

"Jeez-a bloody mi Christi! What I'm-a do to deserve thees? You-a sleep on-a the couch. Now go!" Camellia could be heard apologising to her partner as Pat wandered back to the fire.

The little girl gathered the rug off the floor and as there was a couch in the lounge, she crawled into the unoccupied end. Tony was snoring at the other end. Pat sat for awhile, studying her surroundings. The two men slept on. Pat moved over to Tony, poking a finger into his shoulder. He just mumbled "shlumpf" and feebly brushed at the annoyance. Pat poked again, harder.

"I haven't got my nightie." She stated.

Tony stirred.

"Wassamarra?" He rolled over.

Pat dug at him again. He roused bleary eyes rolling in search of the disturbance.

"I haven't got my nightie." Pat repeated. "Mummy won't let me sleep in my clothes."

"Yes, a nightie." Tony slurred, waking from his drunken stupor.

"Gotta get a nightie." He rolled again and fell on to the floor. It woke him up.

"What's th' matter Camellia?" He looked up and noticed Pat giggling at him.

"What's the matter?" He repeated.

"I got to take my clothes off so I can go to bed and I have not got my nightie."

Pat informed.

"Ah yes. I better put you to bed; le's get your clo's off.

Tony stumbled towards her.

Part Four

Early the next morning Pamela and David crept into Trisha's room. She was wide awake sitting in bed, playing with her toy bear.

"Good morning Dear." Pamela smiled as she kissed Trisha's forehead.

"Uncle David has come to say goodbye, he is off to work soon."

He too, kissed Trisha's forehead.

"See you at dinner-time Love, you be a good girl for Aunt Pamela, won't you?"

Trisha smiled shyly from behind her bear as she nodded vigorously. When Pamela had seen David off from the gate she returned to the house, her heart singing for joy in anticipation of the lovely day ahead of her. A child of her own at last! Well, at least for some time, until Jenny demanded her back. Hopefully that would be a long, long way off. A joyous morning elapsed, Pamela sorting out clothing with Trisha and preparing her shower, brushing the lovely dark curls and pottering in the garden together. As they made sandwiches for lunch, Pamela asked Trisha if the weather was nicer here in Melbourne or better back in Tasmania.

"I don't know Aunt Pamela, I haven't been there."

"Haven't been where Dear?" Pamela asked.

"To that Tas- what you said."

"Tasmania? But Darling, that is where you just came from."

"No Aunt Pamela, I came from Sydney. We lived at Bondi, daddy always walked along the beach with me, we used to gather shells. We - we."

Trisha began to cry. She rushed to Pamela, sobbing into her apron.

"Why did mummy and daddy die? I didn't want them to die!?"

Shocked, Pamela tried to comfort the youngster. A great gnawing dread began to take over her whole being. Dark suspicion was dawning. There was something drastically wrong here; the child was so sure of her facts. Pamela took Trisha to her room and left her sobbing on the bed with an arm around the bear, both covered by a blanket. She frantically rang her husband at his office.

"David, I need you here. Please come home, its, its quite urgent!"

Within fifteen minutes David was entering the house.

"What is it Pet. Is something wrong with Trisha?"

"No. She is well, but - but she is not ours!"

"I know Dear, we've only got a lend of her but surely Jenny doesn't want her back yet; does she?"

"Not that David, she is not our Pat, we have the wrong girl. She said she lived in Sydney - at Bondi - how could Pat know those names?"

David stood stunned.

"You know, I had a suspicion; just a minute."

He went into their bedroom and returned with the name-tag he kept.

"See that Love? Look at the name. There really was a mix-up somewhere!"

They stared hopelessly at the now damning evidence.

"If we have the wrong child, then what she says about her parents being killed could be true. The poor little thing, go up to her David, she misses her dad very much."

Pamela urged her husband. Not a word was spoken when David sat on Trisha's bed, he just reached out and she snuggled her head into his chest. David patted her gently as he kissed her curls. When the sobbing had stopped, Pamela suggested a cup of tea and a glass of milk with biscuits. While the girl was thus engaged, David slipped a pad and pencil out of his coat pocket.

"Trisha, can you write your name for me?" He asked.

She nodded and took the implements. A fairly neat 'Patricia' was the result.

"And your last name too, can you write that?"

She wrote again. 'Lorenza'. David felt his heart sink. He felt he too, could cry. As Pamela placed the tray on the bed-side table, David thanked Trisha and handed the paper to Pamela.

"Oh dear, that is what I was afraid of, something like that." Her eyes glistened. "What are we to do David/"

"We will finish our tea first and then check with the airlines!"

"But David, wait. I - I don't want to lose her, we - we have waited so long. Don't let her go - we won't tell them - I love her so. Please don't send her back."

Pamela was beginning to panic and become hysterical. The thought of losing that precious little being that she had waited so long for, had yearned for, and prayed for; Pamela could not let go now that she had her.

"Darling, not in front of the child, let us go to the kitchen and talk this thing over, come on."

David ushered Pamela out quickly.

"Back in a minute, drink your milk." He forced a smile at Tricia.

In the kitchen, Pamela was frantically trying to think of excuses why they should not return the girl to her rightful guardians. As they were heatedly discussing the situation, Trisha came to the doorway, tears again evident.

"Do I have to go back to Bondi Uncle David? I don't want to, I want to stay, I like it here. Please Aunt Pamela, can't I stay?"

She looked so hopeless and lost in the doorway. Pamela rushed over and embraced her.

"Trisha Dear, you poor little lamb, there has been a mix-up of some sort. We want you to stay but -!"

David placed a finger to his lips.

"Let us not say too much just yet Pet and remember one thing - somewhere or other is a little girl named Pat, belonging to my sister. What has happened to her?"

Part Five

It was a comparatively easy matter to locate the other little girl. When David notified the Airport of the mix-up, he was hard pressed to have them believe him. It could not possibly happen; all children travelling alone were tagged and had an Air Hostess personally deliver them to their correct guardians. No, it was not possible to mix them, not with this airline. However David's persistence won out and the flights of the doubtful times were checked. It was found that indeed there were two little girls of similar names and appearances arriving on closely associated flights. The airline was very apologetic and would send people immediately to sort out this most unfortunate incident. If Mister Lawrence would be so kind as not to make this most regrettable incident public, they would be very grateful.

"Oh, cut the nonsense" David growled "just give me the address of the other girl's guardian and I will take her there myself and pick up my own niece. Just give me the damned address, I don't want any publicity either; it won't help the children!"

"Yes Sir. Well if you would be so kind -!"

The address was duly given. The fact was gently and carefully explained to Trisha that she was with the wrong aunt and uncle but when she was with her real aunt and uncle, she could always come to visit and they would be very happy to have her. Maybe she could even stay some week-ends! It was very hard on the youngster to have found a happy home after losing her parents so suddenly but she was assured that her real aunt and uncle would make her very happy and give her a good home too. Now Trisha would have two lots of relations.

"But I don't have an Uncle - I don't think! Mummy said my Aunt is no good 'cause she won't marry!" Trisha looked up with wide eyes.

"Then why did you say nothing and come with us if you knew you did not have an uncle?" David demanded.

Trisha began to fidget, frowning at her shoes.

"Well, I wasn't sure if I liked you but I missed my Daddy. Uncle David, do I really have to go?"

Pamela was about to speak but David stepped in first.

"Your real aunt will be terribly worried and she has our little girl. You will just be changing over from one nice home to another. What say we pack up and get you nice and neat for your real aunt?"

- -

When Tony reached for Pat, the front door slammed as Camellia's 'guest' left and she entered the lounge room with a smile on her usually sulky features. The cash tucked into her cleavage had brightened her up a little. She would have a hot drink and then go to bed, enough work for tonight. She beheld Tony hovering over little Pat.

"Hey you bast! What-a you do?"

Tony sheepishly staggered around.

"'Ullo Love, th' chi - child wan's a go bed. Gotta get her clo's orf!"

Camellia kicked Antonio in the leg.

"Ah! You stupid-a bloody drunks. I'm-a fix it. Antonio, wake you up!"

She kicked him again. He stirred.

"Right-o, right-o, who's shout?"

"Its-a no shout - you go - pees off!"

Antonio struggled to his feet and lurched out as Tony subsided on the couch again.

Camellia took Pat out the back and then settled her into a make-shift bed on the kitchen couch. Camellia was a little gentler now that she had finished her beat and was cashed up. As the little girl slept, Camellia pondered upon ways to rid herself of the unwanted mill-stone, the while she sipped coffee. When Pat awoke the next morning, she had no idea it was eleven o'clock as she could not read the time. She had slept well because of the exhausting day of terrors that befell her and also the fact that she was not properly bedded down until almost midnight. The rest of the household was quiet as Pat looked about at the un-familiar surroundings, her small mind trying to piece together why she was away from mummy and what the future would be. Pat was unhappy here, she hated the place, she was also hungry. Getting up, the little girl took off the over-sized singlet that Camellia had put her into and she dressed herself. Her clothes were hanging on a kitchen chair. In the lounge, she tip-toed past Tony who had fallen off the couch again but was still sound asleep on the floor amid an array of cans and bottles. Pat pushed the front bedroom door open and peered in cautiously. The door creaked and Camellia stirred. She rolled over and opened her eyes. The two watched each other silently, and then Camellia said.

"So, you up. Come-a here."

Pat bit her lip as she timidly crossed the room.

"I theenk you-a like to-a go to nice orphanage, is-a lots of kids to-a play with. Eh! Sounds good, no?"

Pat did not really know what Camellia was talking about but it must be better than here, so she nodded.

"Ha. It's-a beuno. I'm-a get some breakfast!"

She dressed and they went to the kitchen, Camellia kicking Tony awake as she passed, calling.

"Get it up, lazy pig!"

Breakfast was actually brunch and Camellia cooked a solid meal of sausages, chops and vegetables. It was a lazy affair as they usually did nothing all day. Camellia earned their money by night.

Part Six

By two o'clock Camellia was ready with Pat's bag packed and they were both dressed to leave, when a knock sounded at the door. She opened it to find the Lawrence's there with Trisha.

"Yes?" Camellia enquired.

David introduced himself, Pamela and Trisha, explaining there was a mix-up with the children. Could they come in and talk? Camellia frowned as she ushered them in, apologising for the mess.

"I'm-a no clean up yet. What you say - mix-up?"

David pushed the un-willing Trisha forwards as he tried to explain.

"This is Trisha, she is your niece, we have to give her back to you and -?"

"Ah no you-a don't" Camellia almost screamed "I got it one kid I'm-a no want, you don'-a give me no more!"

"No, you do not understand. This little girl is your Trisha!"

Camellia pulled Pat from behind her and pushed the girl forwards.

"I got it one Trisha, I'm-a no want more!"

Pamela spoke up.

"No, that is our Trisha - I mean Pat. You see they are both named Patricia and you got our Pat by mistake!"

"Sure is-a mistake. Eef she your Trisha you take. I'm-a no want, I take it to Orph'nage."

Camellia pushed Pat to the Lawrence's and hustled them all out, shouting.

"Eef it's-a you kid take it and go. Out, out!"

She slammed the door behind them. David and Pamela stood nonplussed. The two girls wailed in unison.

"What the hell -?" David expostulated.

"The children first dear - get them in the car - we'll talk it over!"

91

Pamela urged, leading the way. She bundled the two girls into the back seat and got in with them. David sat in the front seat, scratching his head.

Pamela dried Trisha's eyes with her handkerchief then applied it to the other waif, so ingloriously thrust upon them. As she dabbed at the child's cheeks, Pamela asked.

"Is your name Pat Lawrence, Dear?"

Pat nodded.

"Oh I am so glad!" Pamela sighed as she studied the girl.

"Yes, I can see you are a Lawrence. Oh Darling. I am your aunt Pamela and you are going to live with us now, everything will be fine."

Pat watched the kindly face through wet eyes and sobbed softly as Pamela stroked her hair.

"That's it Dear, have a good cry now you understand, that is not a nice place to live is it?"

Trisha burst forth again.

"I don't want to live there either; you don't want me now you've got her!"

The racket was too much for David.

"Good grief, it's all yours, I am getting out."

Just as he alighted and closed the car door, Tony came from the house with Pat's suitcase.

"Hey! You'll need this." He called.

"Oh yes, nearly forgot that." David went and retrieved the small suitcase.

"Your Trisha is in the car, I'll fetch her for you."

"What are you talking about, we don't want any kids, you can 'ave her."

"We have our niece and we have returned your girl - she is your family - you will have to take her."

"She ain't my fam'ly, b'longs to Camellia only she don't want the kid neither. Was takin' her to th' orphanage when you came. The kid's parents are dead and we got landed with her, can't you take her?"

Tony dropped the case by David's feet as he spoke.

"But dammit man, you can't treat a child like a piece of merchandise. There are legalities to attend - papers to sign - adoption arrangements!"

"Arrgh, for Chrissake. If you want th' kid, take her, we'll sign th' papers!"

Tony stormed back into the house. David placed the case on the front seat beside him when he got back into the car and sat thinking. Trisha was still sobbing but Pat was quiet.

"Well Dear, what happened, what do we do with Trisha?"

"How do you feel about having two nieces?"

"David?" Pamela gasped.

"Two nieces, you mean, both of them. Pat and Trisha - two Patricia's?"

David nodded a huge grin on his face.

Realisation slowly dawned upon Trisha's tortured mind.

"Truly Uncle David, you really truly mean it - please?"

Her little body shivered. Pamela leaned over and kissed her.

"We will be one big happy family and you both have a sister now. How is that, we will all love each other!"

David returned to check fully with Camellia and tell her of their decision. Camellia was actually smiling as she waved them goodbye. David lit and puffed contentedly upon his pipe. Pamela was in an excited conversation with two very happy little girls.

THE END.

© Howard Reede-Pelling.

Preface
Laurie

A tale of two no-hopers typical of some current teenagers who are just grab-what-you-can merchants, they have no regard to what belongs to others.

ATTENTION! Gutter language and sexual references are to be found in this story.

This tale is entirely fictional and any reference to people alive or deceased is purely co-incidental.

The Author **Howard Reede-Pelling** claims exclusive rights and no other person has any right to copy, either electronically or otherwise, any part or portion of this story.

Laurie

Laurie hated cops they were a bloody nuisance, always interfering and snooping about when a bloke wanted to do anything; especially when you wanted to try and make a few dollars. He furtively looked about now as the house he had selected earlier came within view, it was dark now and the place looked as if it was deserted; Laurie had a final quick glance down the dark street and seeing no movement of any sort entered the front garden. A stealthy few steps had him hidden from possible sight behind a handy shrub which was covering a window that he had selected at his final appraisal of the house in the daylight earlier that day. So far everything was going to plan, all was quiet and there appeared to be no one at home; this should be easy - he thought. Carefully prising open the window with the screw driver he had brought along for the purpose, Laurie eased his lanky frame through the aperture now available to him. All was quiet except when he stood upon the floor, there was a distinct squeak - shit - Laurie stood still; listening. All appeared serene; he stealthily looked about the darkened room which was slightly illuminated by the glow from a little light in a smoke detector upon the ceiling. This was the lounge room and other than heavy furniture and quite exotic looking vases, nothing of value that could be easily taken and disposed of was about. Laurie crept noiselessly to the door and carefully peered about. Deserted, the passageway was clear and the door opposite would be the master bedroom, which is where anything of value would be kept. As he peered in he noticed two humps on the bed, the house was indeed occupied; Laurie had to be careful. On a bedside chair he found a pair of men's trousers and silently rifled the pockets, the notes he shoved into his own pocket and took out a small folder of credit cards - they too were stuffed into his pocket. Silently easing open one of the drawers of a bedside table he quickly went through the drawers; finding nothing he could see as valuable Laurie glanced at the two humps as he quit the room.

Gliding along the passageway again he gave the children's room a miss - there would only be trouble from there and nothing to gain - the kitchen would have food and drink available. Laurie was rifling through the pantry and stuffing cheese and a handful of biscuits down his shirt, very disappointed that there were no cigarettes about; when a shrill voice piped from the doorway.

"Hey! Whatcha doing in my house?" It was a seven year old boy dressed in his pyjamas. Laurie quickly went to the boy and covered his mouth to prevent further noise; he dragged his unwilling victim to the back door and tried to escape that way.

"Fuck!" He muttered as the deadlock held.

The boy was a hindrance as he struggled to get clear and Laurie cast him aside and attempted to unlatch the door, the lock was unfamiliar to him so he desisted with it and grabbed a bottle from the kitchen sink and smashed the window with it to escape that way. As he was struggling through the window the light illuminated and a male voice raged.

"You stinking bloody thief, take that!"

That was a kitchen stool cast by a wrathful owner at a thief trying to escape him. The heavy stool hit Laurie fair in the back as he was silhouetted in the window by the moonlight. The force of the blow knocked the wind out of Laurie as he fell to the ground outside. He was gasping and trying to regain his breath when a heavy hand grabbed his wind-proof coat and held him back. Laurie quickly rid himself of the coat and got to his feet; he raced away not even looking back to see if he was being followed. The home owner was still leaning out of the window with the coat in his grasp and a snivelling son being comforted by his mother. Laurie put as much distance as he could between himself and the scene of his misdemeanour, panting heavily from his exertions the thief gained the comparative safety of a park and went through his spoils. One hundred and eighty-five dollars in cash and a small pocket satchel of credit cards, he grinned to himself as he chewed at the lump of cheese - slightly the worse for wear - that he had scored. 'Have to nick up to an ATM and get a couple of hundred out before they notify the bank about the stolen cards', Laurie thought to himself, 'the damn bank will be a trap to try now that I was caught getting the stuff - damn it - might be thousands in their account 'cause they seemed to be a rich lot'.

Laurie finished the cheese and began upon the biscuits as he hurried to the nearest outlet to relieve the man's account of another couple of hundred dollars. He knew of an ATM up at the shopping centre and there would be no one about at this time of night, Laurie hurried to it and after trying a few combinations that were ineffective; kicked the machine.

"Bloody hell!" He raved. "Should have taken his bloody wallet, some silly buggers have their code numbers in a hidden pocket or something - ah - I'll nick over to Slim's joint and see if I can flog the cards for a couple a' hundred!"

He slapped the ATM again and headed for Slim's. As Laurie made his way to try and get some sort of gain from his night's work, he went down an alley way where two dead-beats were lounging; he thought he could just pass without being accosted. How wrong he was, they confronted him.

"Give us y' dough!" The larger of the two threatened.

"Ain't got none."

Laurie made to pass; he was roughly manhandled and firmly held by the large man as the other went through his pockets. The cash and cards were taken from him and Laurie was shoved to the ground and received a hefty kick in the ribs, as he lay there gasping for breath the two assailants walked away; as unconcerned as if they were just going for a stroll. Painfully the injured young thief struggled to his feet.

"I'll get even with the buggers." Laurie mumbled to himself as he tried to recollect as much as he could of the two muggers. He found a telephone booth just around the corner and rang the emergency number. When it was answered he just mentioned that a house had been robbed and the two offenders were in the vicinity of the shopping centre, Laurie gave a brief description of the two who had robbed him of his ill-gotten gains and hung up.

"Hope they get nicked for robbing me now!"

Laurie grinned as he went on to Slim's place.

The night was still dark when Laurie arrived at his destination, Slim would still be asleep and as he often visited this guy the disgruntled ruffian opened the back door and walked in; as he had done many times before. Slim was in dreamland so Laurie made himself some coffee and sat at the table sipping the beverage, his thoughts were dark concerning the thugs that had taken his nights work.

"Bastards" he muttered "I hope the cops get 'em - should do if they respond to that tip-off I gave 'em, if the pigs get on to it right away they'll cop 'em; they weren't in no hurry."

He sat muddling over what to do next to get a couple of dollars. The kitchen doorway was befouled by Slim as he appeared dressed only in his underpants.

"Smelled the coffee so I thought it musta been you, any coffee left?"

A bleary-eyed young ruffian also in his late teens grinned.

"The water's still hot!" Laurie said as he nodded towards the kettle. "Just got 'ere after I did a job on an 'ouse over the other side 'a the park, got a fair swag a' dollars an' some credit cards but a couple of bloody big hoods sprung me as I was comin' 'ere wiv th' stuff - but I got even with 'em - still I'm broke but; bloody arse'oles!"

Laurie grumbled as he spat out the venom.

"Ay! I'm gonna chuck on some clothes an' go up to the arcade, there was a grouse little bitch there th' other day playing the machines, she gimme the eye; reckon I'll score wiv her. D'ya wanna come?" Slim eagerly grinned.

"Not a dark haired girl with a thick layer of paint on was she?" Laurie frowned.

"Yair, but she's a good looker!" Slim enthused.

"I don't want nuthin' t' do with her - she's a slut!" Laurie informed. "I might as well come wiv ya though, ain't nuthin' t' do just hanging about here."

The two sauntered in to the Pin-Ball Arcade and looked about, Slim seeking his fancy and Laurie wanting to know just who was there - maybe even the great oafs that diddled him out of his night's work; he did not think so though - they were too old for this caper. There were not many people in there this early, just a couple of kids playing one of the machines.

"Ain't no one 'ere, c'mon; let's nick over to the park there should be a couple 'a Sheila's there or sumpin'". Slim surmised.

When the two got within view of their destination they were disappointed.

"Bloody hell, it's too early th' place is deserted!" Laurie moaned.

"Well we can sit on the swings for a bit an' have a yakker, someone'll turn up soon." Slim proceeded to the swings. Half an hour later the two were still grizzling about the fact that it was too early for their mates or any 'snotty-nosed' little urchins for that matter, to be about and it was getting too damned cold just waiting out in the open anyway.

"C'mon Laurie, lets nick orf t' the township, there will be more to do where the shops are anyway." Slim led the way, so Laurie followed.

The township appeared just as deserted as the park was, absolutely nobody about.

"Ah, what a shit of a hick-joint this here bloody town is; there's nuthin' t' do an' the rotten shops are all closed - what time is it anyway?" Laurie asked.

"Dunno, the town hall clock is just aroun' the corner, I'll nick up an' see." He did so.

"Gee, no wonder a bloke's moanin' it's only seven in the morning."

"Yeah, it is getting' late - what say we try an' pry open the damn ATM?"

Laurie suggested. Slim looked doubtful.

"S'pose we could try but there's sure t' be people goin' to work soon, I don't reckon we'll get anythin' an' we'd make too much of a racket and we ain't got no tools."

Laurie had a brainwave.

"What say we do over a coupla cars, maybe the owners'l still be asleep or havin' brekky.

"Now you're talkin', an' I know just th' street where they's a coupla BMW's".

He led the way at a brisk trot, Laurie quickly followed. When they reached the street, sure enough there were two of the prized vehicles parked and no one about; the two quickly got to work checking all the doors first and finding no easy ingress attacked the windows with the rolled up coat hanger that Slim always carried. He straightened it out then bent it to slide down the glass window and wiggled it to lift the rod which released the door. They went through the glove box, the interior and all the pockets of the doors. Behind one of the seats Laurie found a brief case, while from the glove box Slim managed to locate a pair of ear rings; they abandoned that vehicle and attacked the other BMW. This one was very clean, nothing to be gained by ransacker's; they left it quickly just as the owner came from his residence.

"You stinking bloody thieves!" He yelled as he charged at them.

The two frightened teenagers fairly flew in panic and were lost to view in seconds. The distraught owner used his mobile telephone to call the authorities.

Meanwhile, Laurie and Slim were still high tailing it to the park where they took stock of their spoils.

"Wonder 'ow much 'ol get fer these 'ere jools, must be worf 'eaps by th' look a them?"

Slim queried.

Meanwhile Laurie was going through the brief case.

"Just bloody papers!" He moaned. "Ay, wait a sec', this looks good!"

He withdrew a cheque. "Strewth!" He gasped. "It's for Three Thousand Dollars, 'ow c'n I cash in on it?" He looked in wonder at his accomplice.

"Ya sure? Wot about takin' it t' Len th' forger. He might know somethin'; you'll 'ave ter give 'im half but it's better'n nuffin'. "E might give me a deal on these 'ere jools too.

Slim smugly suggested.

"Yair, good idea, let's nick over to 'im right away."

They proceeded to Len the forger. When they arrived at his shop it was not open.

"Argh! It's only eight o'clock,'e don't open 'til nine, we'll 'ave ter wait!" Slim grumbled.

They sat down in front of the shop to await it's opening. A police car pulled up and two policemen got out, they walked up to the youths.

"Did you young fellows see a couple of older men around about here this morning?"

The younger of the policemen inquired, giving more description of the two that assaulted Laurie earlier.

"Yair, they was down Lassenger Lane 'an they went off in the direction of th' shopping centre!" Laurie informed, not explaining that it was he who put in the report.

The officers nodded their thanks and got back in their car. They left. Both boys grinned their relief as the police departed.

"Gee, I thought we were goners then." Slim breathed a sigh of relief.

"Yair." Laurie nodded."

Ten minutes later that same police car travelled past again, it kept going but in it were the two thugs that robbed Laurie of his night's work. Laurie slapped his cohort on the back.

"Ay, them's the two buggers wot robbed me!"

They were still discussing their misdemeanour's ten minutes later when that same police car returned. The officers stepped out once more.

"It's a funny thing you know" - one of them spoke - "one of those two blokes we apprehended did have the stolen credit cards on him but said that they took them off a bloke answering your description." He looked keenly at Laurie. "You also fit the description of an intruder into a house that was burgled and we have received another bulletin about two cars that were also broken into; you two are under arrest."

Both Slim and Laurie gritted their teeth with disgust at their stupidity in just waiting for a 'fence' and ended up with a lot more to worry about.

The End.

Gold Digger

A rather wealthy man who has been two-timed by his wife seeks his essential needs from a 'street girl', he becomes infatuated by her and believes she could be changed from her present calling and be made a lady. The pitfalls of her former way of life are difficult for them to overcome, many are the problems that they have to better.

Drugs and brutality are heavily depicted with some rather heavy language and sordid situations. This is not advisable reading for youngsters or impressionable teenagers.

Gold Digger   Begun April 2013 Finished 5/1/2015.

She was only a tart really, well you could see that just by looking at her, the jaunty walk and scanty attire that was her means to attract a few wolf whistles; mind you she certainly was pretty - well underneath all of the paint which was liberally applied to those good looks. Beryl did not seem to have the nous to know that the passer-by could tell that she had no principals at all, she was just another trollop with her bare backside quite visible through her very short, tight-fitting jeans shorts and the very pronounced bosoms bursting through her low cut bodice as if they too, were ashamed of where they were and were attempting to escape their predicament.

Beryl exposed a very forced smile that had no humour in it to the passing throng, her lovely white teeth seemed to outdo her very sordid attempt to be a 'good girl' and a lout picking up cigarette butts, gave her a surly glance as she traipsed on by him. Of course Beryl ignored the hopeless person knowing that he would have no money, a thing that she adored and was desperate for; there must be a prospect soon that would accost her. Beryl was looking to the passing limousines for a rich 'hit', someone with money would only be found in the nicer suburbs, she was making her way there now.

This was the suburb to which she was aspiring, South Yarra, yes the hoy-polloy suburb of Melbourne; here is where Beryl knew that people had the wealth to be interested enough to want a 'girlie' for sex. This was a one-time slum area but now-through development, the slums had gone and new town houses had ousted all the low rental people away. It was now a prosperous and desired area for business people and the elite that was very close to the large metropolis of Melbourne. As Beryl flounced her way along the shopping strip of Toorak Road, her luck improved as a very new and smart Audi cruised into the gutter beside her and the window was wound down. A smart looking executive type smiled at her and tilted his head with a query. Without a word Beryl opened the door and made herself comfortable, the sedan whisked her away.

Beryl lowered her bodice fractionally to expose more of her ample bosom then brushed her hair into place as she glanced into the interior mirror; satisfied she studied her escort. He was smiling at her as she noticed that his eyes had been focussed upon her shapely body.

"Your place or a motel?" She enquired.

"Does it matter?" He asked.

"No, it can be the local park for all I care. Was her flippant answer.

"The Lazy Bods Motel is not far away, we will try that - want a shower?"

Beryl shrugged but said nothing.

The motel was a little way out of town but Beryl did not mind that, not in this fine limousine. It was a most gorgeous day and the drive was quite exhilarating with the beautiful countryside to witness as they motored smoothly along. Soon the motel appeared and the young man entered reception, acquired the key and led his prize into the fairly opulent premises of this out-of-the-way quality motel. Beryl was impressed, this was not one of your average run-of-the-mill motels but a place of respectability; they indulged themselves in their intimate pastime and both were equally satisfied with the outcome. Beryl was placing her rather large earnings within the comfort of her bosom and made to get back into the limousine; when her companion stayed her.

"What is the rush honey?" He asked.

Surprised, Beryl turned to the greying middle aged man.

"You are going to drive me back aren't you?"

"Eventually, but not yet, I need some lunch, won't you accompany me?"

"Oh! I was not expecting that - do I get extra for it?

"If you must - sure - I can accommodate you, but I wish to discuss a proposition and I was hoping that you would be interested in it; come into the dining room and we'll have a gourmet lunch!" His engulfing smile had her intrigued, Beryl allowed him to take her by the arm.

The two were ushered to a table where a wine was poured for them but what man wanted to discuss with her had the young lady piqued. While they sipped wine the waiter took their lunch orders. Beryl waited expectantly, what this smart good-looking man wanted, had her raise an eyebrow expectantly. Her escort studied Beryl evidently trying to find the right words to express his next remark.

"I really enjoyed our time back there - how was it for you?" He asked.

"Okay, but what has that got to do with anything, it was just another job!" Beryl supplied.

"I was wondering if you would like it to be a regular job, could we carry it on as a more permanent position; weekly at least?" He eyed her expectantly.

Beryl raised her eyebrows, pursed her lips and then offered.

"Sure, suits me; regularity is good. When and what time, same day I suppose?"

"No I was thinking more of an evening and we could arrange another nice dinner."

"Won't your wife get in the way of an evening?" Beryl was trying to avoid possible trouble.

"No worries there, I just got through a divorce settlement; I am a free spirit now!"

Beryl again raised her eyebrows and was pondering her escort's intentions. Was this a trick of some sort or was he legitimate, had he really been divorced or was this just talk to lure her into a dirty deception; Beryl had no desire to be caught up in any legal trap. The middle aged man seemed to divine her thoughts and tried to put her mind at rest.

"There is no need to worry, I truly am a free spirit now and very glad to be out of the commitment I was pushed into; you see I am rather well off – so is my ex – and she just happened to be smitten by a billionaire and wanted to be rid of me. It suited me fine for when I became aware that she was two-timing me I was devastated and to avoid a costly separation we both mutually agreed to just part amicably, which we did about two months ago – so you see; I am now at a loose end. What about we give it a try for a couple of weeks and if we are compatible; well, one never knows!" He peered at her critically. She responded off handed.

"Yeah, we will give it a go but you had better not be getting me involved in anything tricky; I have some heavies I can rely on if you are!"

"I will meet you in the 'Comfort Bar' at the Casino about eight-thirty on Friday evening, just ask for an ordered table named for Jerry, which is my name – Jerry Thorn-dyke – what is your name Beryl?"

"I don't let my jobs interfere with my privacy, wait a few weeks and if you really are legit, well you never know, can we leave it at that?" Beryl eyed her escort with a frown.

"Good enough, we will leave it at that then; see you on Friday!"

He settled with her and they parted after he dropped her off where he picked her up.

Beryl gazed after his limousine when he drove away. Thoughts of whether she wanted to be involved in a more permanent way wandered willy-nilly through her mind, did she think she could have any deeper feelings for him – he seemed to be a gentleman and he wasn't rough at all – time would give her more of an idea about him. Beryl nodded to herself as she felt of the spoils she had won. There were no friends of hers about this suburb and as she had a quite large sum as payment for her new association, Beryl thought it a good idea to pop into a convenient cafe' and sip on a coffee. She was frowned upon as she sat in a secluded corner to drink and ponder the proposition that she had received, all oblivious of the occasional sultry looks that were cast in her direction. The clientele no doubt thinking that this cafe' was too good for such an obvious tart. Beryl ignored those that thought ill of her so immersed in her own thoughts was she, as she sipped upon her beverage.

'Jerry Thorn-dyke' she mulled over the name, huh, it certainly appeared to be a swell sort of name and was well in keeping with its' owner. If as he said he really was at a loose end momentarily, perhaps this was a great chance for her to by-pass the smutty world in which she found herself? Beryl wondered if it would really last or would she be cast aside when the novelty of a new girl wore off Jerry. He most certainly was very good company when they indulged themselves - and as she had previously thought to herself, the man really was a gentleman the way he treated her; if she played her cards right this man may even be a boon to her. Beryl finished her coffee and quit the cafe', to the evident delight of everybody attending.

On the evening of her appointment with Jerry Thorn-dyke, Beryl was approaching the Casino with the intention of enquiring for the whereabouts of the 'comfort bar', when she was accosted by two fairly well-dressed men. They surrounded her, one at either side and urged her towards a respectable vehicle which was parked nearby. It was a fairly frightened 'street-girl' who was forced into this unknown person's car.

"What's the idea?" Beryl managed to ask, her fear showing.

"Just shut up and don't be any trouble!" She was ordered.

The limousine eased away and leisurely headed for an unknown destination, it purred along the free-way effortlessly. Beryl, resigned to her fate, just enjoyed the ride. She pondered her situation. A frown troubled her forehead.

'These men were strangers to her but they were so far, not really aggressive, so their mission was no doubt to whisk her away somewhere to be interrogated. Now, was it connected with Jerry Thorn-dyke - it seemed possible as she was supposed to be meeting him - maybe he wanted to assure himself that she would do the right thing by him; they appeared to be well-to-do, maybe he wanted to check her out? It seemed to be logical as he was very well off and these two men were in a chauffeured vehicle so perhaps that was the scenario.' Beryl nodded to herself believing she had surmised correctly. Presently the vehicle turned off the free way and drove a kilometre or so until it came to a very opulent homestead, Beryl assumed that she was right in her assumption and very interestedly looked about at what she assumed was Jerry's home. It was not!

The curious 'street girl' was ushered into the homestead and taken to a very large room in which a fire blazed merrily as if welcoming her into the house. A smartly dressed, somewhat corpulent middle-aged gentleman was sitting in an arm chair reading as they entered.

"This is the 'girlie' you ordered is it not Mister 'Q'? We followed her and she agreed to come with us at the Casino?" The more senior of her escorts asked.

Mister 'Q' glanced at the girl over his pince-nez spectacles, Beryl raised her eyebrows in amazement, for this man she recalled was sitting at a table with a quite 'common' type of female in the cafe' where she had taken a coffee in Toorak Road. Now Beryl was beginning to be alarmed as Jerry had no idea that she would take a coffee at that shop; it was after he had gone that she decided to have the refreshment.

When Beryl realised that these men had no connections with Jerry Thorn-dyke, she began to feel quite alarmed.

Meanwhile, at the Casino, Jerry Thorn-dyke was patiently awaiting Beryl for he believed that she was interested enough in his proposal to at least come for the free meal that he had promised. Beryl did not turn up! Jerry was very disappointed as he glanced about hopefully, the waiter approached and asked did he wish to order yet? Jerry did so as he eventually gave up hope that the young lady that he was awaiting would not honour their agreement. He dined alone. Deep down Jerry felt a trace of loneliness for he had great hopes that Beryl could be lured into becoming a lady of some respectability; after a little cosmetic tutoring and regular course of manners. Alas his dreams were shattered and he would have to re-think his future.

Back at the home of 'Mister Q', Beryl was stoical as she awaited her fate. The heavies of the rather plump gentleman were ordered to leave and Mister Q beckoned Beryl over as he ogled at her ample bosom. She stood before him, head held high and a look of expectation upon her over-painted features.

"You know what you are here for I presume?"

The slimy smile was forced.

"I can guess, but why the 'heavies', it is a crime to kidnap people you know? If I had a gun I may have killed them, they are strangers as are you - who are you anyway?

"Quinton is the name but you may call me Olly! I will reimburse you well for your time so there is no need to panic, I noticed you in the cafe' the other day and then had my men follow you; I need to know with whom I am dealing."

"Did it ever occur to you that I may not be interested in working for someone who just takes what they want, I do have some principles you know!"

Beryl was fuming at the audacity of this man who assumed that street girls could be just taken for granted.

"No, I never gave it a thought. You should be honoured that I even noticed a trollop like you - for that I will just use you and then my men can have their way with you and toss you out with the rest of the rubbish!" His oily smile rankled Beryl.

"You calling me trash? Huh, you are just a petty criminal with lots of cash, you are worse than we ladies of the night; at least we earn our money honestly!"

"Enough! While you are here you will do as I ask of you or my friends will see that you are marked so as to be an undesirable pick-up for anyone. Do I make myself clear?" He glared at Beryl with a sickly curl of his lips. Realising that she was at his mercy, the frightened girl thought better of aggravating the man further; she changed tack.

"Well it is just another job - you won't be rough will you, if you take me back safely - then I will do your wishes; just be a little gentle with me!"

Olly enlarged his sickly smile and crooned with a satisfied gloating at Beryl. She flippantly shrugged as she prepared for his advances.

"That is a much better attitude young lady, now if you will come a little closer perhaps we may become more intimate?" He smiled his rather sickly pleasure.

Beryl did as she was bid, he began fondling her breasts with a happy grin.

After a while he gently took her by the hand and ushered his prize into the bedroom where he got his satisfaction; then returned to the lounge.

"Would you care for a drink and some refreshments?"

He was now sexually sated and appeared to be somewhat a changed person, for Olly appeared to be a changed man from the person that Beryl had first met.

"Yes thanks, that would be great - er - you will have me returned to the Casino; won't you?" Beryl was wide-eyed as she asked, for this man was an uncertain quantity, liable to have a change of heart at any moment she thought.

"Yes my dear, you will be properly recompensed too, I did enjoy myself and as you behaved well then you will be looked after!"

He rang a little bell on a table at hand. A steward appeared.

"A nice red and some nibbles Jules." The steward bowed and left.

Beryl was sent back to the casino with a payment and was very satisfied after the initial fright, she had left a telephone number at Olly's request so as it would be easy for him to contact her again. The number was that of her rooming house that was used when she had a prospect to accommodate. Beryl was at pains not to have her private premises known to her clients, she was always wary of being followed home; it was dangerous for one with her way of life to be vulnerable like that. Her privacy was her only salvation.

It was the following Friday evening and Beryl was standing at the Casino again, wondering whether she should enter and look for 'The Comfort Bar' where she was supposed to be a week before. Would Jerry attend this Friday? She wondered if he was a regular or not, perhaps it was just a thought on the night. Beryl attempted to enter but was refused by the attendant at the door.

"Sorry Miss, ladies of the street are not permitted in the Casino, unless they are accompanied by a member; just walk on by please."

He motioned her away.

"But I am expected by Mister Thorn-dyke, he is waiting at the Comfort Bar for me!" The doorman glanced at a sheet he took from a pocket.

"Sorry Miss, Mister Thorn-dyke is not expecting anyone tonight, he has not even placed a name for a visitor as he has not come here tonight; good evening miss." Again he waved her off.

Beryl began to walk off when a motor horn was lightly sounded beside her as a limousine that she recognised stopped at the drop-off point. Jerry had the window down as he waved Beryl in, surprised, she did so and they motored off leaving the doorman perplexed.

"I decided to return tonight just in case you did show up." Jerry stated as they entered the Casino car parking area for clients. "Just as well I did, what happened last week - did you have second thoughts?"

Beryl pondered what to answer, she decided to be truthful to Jerry knowing that he would eventually find out and anyway, she was a 'street girl' after all and he knew that. If as he said, there could be something in it for her - well - it would be better in the long run if indeed Jerry was serious about the future. She nodded to herself as she pouted before replying.

"I was snatched by a couple of heavies as I waited for you, they took me away to another client; I was afraid I might have been scarred if I hadn't done what they wanted. They didn't do nuthin' to me because their boss was in a cafe' I went to after I left you the other night and he had them follow me; they picked me up when I was waiting for you!" Beryl watched closely for Jerry's reaction.

"With your calling things like that are bound to happen, this is the reason why I want to change your life style. That is the very reason that this evening is all about, will you give me a chance to get you out of this way of life? Here we are now and when we are having our meal we will discus things together, you will be more welcome here at the Casino when I have had some people give you a proper make-up and get all that over-painted rubbish off you; make your beautiful features more life-like. Will you let me do this and when you are more like a lady of fashion - well - then life will begin for you with a new outlook and fine clothing and a few pointers about etiquette; why you will be a lady of some substance and I will be really proud to have you beside me!"

Her surprised look at him made Jerry smile and nod happily, he ushered her to a seat at the table he had reserved and they settled comfortably. The waiter took their orders. Jerry had a huge engulfing smile upon his face as he addressed her.

"Well Beryl, are you ready to hear what I have in mind in more detail? This may be quite a shock to you, I intend to change your lifestyle enormously, it may be a little hard for you to comprehend you know."

Jerry sat with a cheery face and a wistful smile as he watched his partner. With raised eyebrows Beryl stated rather guardedly.

"You are serious aren't you?" Her frown was in wonder at his statement.

"Oh yes, my word I am serious. In the past week I have given this matter a great deal of my time wondering just what the risk would be for me to culminate this outlandish idea of mine, then I thought back of my wife and her two-timing schemes towards me; it broke my heart when I finally came to grips with her duplicity. Then I remembered the pleasure I got when we enjoyed our time together, you and I, that is when I began to come to grips with the idea of making a lady of you - I had my misgivings you know but I sensed that you could be a changed person if given the best opportunity to get out of the rat-race in which you are embroiled. I want your honest opinion Beryl; are you willing to give it a try?" He looked at her with caring eyes and a worried frown.

"I know I am taking a huge risk in even asking a lady of the streets to change her ways, still I feel a great empathy towards you and I believe that we could become a loving couple given a little time to get to know each other better; are you willing to give away your present lifestyle if I help you to acclimatise?" It was an eye opener for Beryl, she sat spellbound looking at him.

The waiter delivered their meals which gave Beryl a little time to analyse this amazing proposition put to her. She was silent as they began their repast. That her life style would be changed enormously Beryl had no doubt, could she cope with that change had Beryl pondering. Jerry was really in earnest she could see that, as he sat awaiting an answer to his question his smiling face took her all in and the man was like a youth on pins and needles all agog with hope.

"You know, I have been really thinking about this sort of an opportunity to get a better lifestyle, if I do try to change, you won't leave me in the lurch will you? It would break my heart if you just used me for a couple of months and then threw me out. I really haven't had a decent life you know, I was barely dragged up as a teenager and had a very brutal step father who had no scruples what-so-ever. I am not used to a steady relationship and may not be able to cope; you know?" Her very worried brow gave Jerry to understand that Beryl was in two minds about this great alteration to her life that he was trying to entice her to make. Jerry took one of her hands and caressed it with feeling. His very honest face had a spark of enthusiasm about it as he tried to reassure this fairly new acquaintance of his, that he only had her best interests in mind and that he would be there for her no matter what; providing that she was true to him and left her sordid life style behind. He avowed that from this day on a new future beckoned with tantalising realism that indeed would be no flash in the pan! Beryl studied his open face and had made up her mind to at least give this splendid opportunity a trial, she cautiously asked.

"What will happen if I slip and forget, I may just automatically go with the next client that accosts me?"

"Then that would tell me that you are not committed to this challenge, I will need for you to give it your best shot, this is a once-in-a-lifetime chance for you to become a lady of some substance, you must be totally honest with me for this is not going to be cheap; it will cost a lot to have you transformed into being a real lady. By the time I have had you beautified, properly groomed and dressed, then get you instructed in the proper behaviour for one in the standing of high society, supply you with your own personal transport and allow you a hand-maid or personal assistant; well, the sky may be the limit!"

Jerry let Beryl think about that for a little while, she may need time to think about the commitment she would be letting herself into. Beryl nodded to herself and pondered a little longer; then cautiously asked.

"I am warming to the enormity of this great opportunity that you have thrust upon me, Jerry, do you really think we can do it? I am really frightened that I will not cope you know - it is just a - well; a Cinderella transformation you are asking of me - I, I just don't know if I can do it!" Her eyes appealed.

"We will not rush into things right away, let us concentrate upon enjoying this evening and get our heads together - er - are you ready for your sweets course yet?" He grinned and tried to get Beryl at ease.

She nodded with a wry smile and Jerry ordered their sweets course.

"You know" he began "I really think you will enjoy the lifestyle that I have in mind for you - you are really a most beautiful girl under all of that paint - it is just not you to be flirting your way through this sordid way of life with it's uncertainties and I know, there must be a great deal of pitfalls for you; I would like for you as of this moment to forget the past and think only of this glorious opportunity for you to become a person of some substance. You can do it - we can and will - make a good thing of it for both of us; please be a good kid for me Beryl and give it a chance to work for us!" His worried face pleaded.

She stopped eating and looked deeply into his eyes, the spoonful of sweets remained resting upon the dish, as she gently nodded.

"Yes, we will give it a trial - but remember - be a little patient with me, it is going to be quite an effort for me; I do not know if I will be able to just drop my present way of life!"

"That's the girl, together we will make this work for the both of us, I am sick and tired of having the future manipulated by an untrue partner; I truly am hoping that a girl like yourself who has been through the mill will relish a proper relationship with an honest partner. You really will be true to me?"

Jerry had a slight frown upon his open face and Beryl could not but doubt his real sincerity, the boyish looks and genuine openness of this rather handsome man gave her a feeling that was very hard for her to subscribe to; laying out a future that she had secretly aspired to but thought was out of her reach.

Chapter Two

Mister Q was frowning at his underling, they were in his opulent games room standing at the billiards table, the subject of their conversation was Beryl; the street girl that Mister Q had used one-time.

"Well she can't be far away, just because she is not answering her telephone does not mean she has skipped out!" Olly Quinton suggested.

"She is probably on an all-night stand with some pick-up or another Boss, do you want that we should cruise around a bit and see if we can fluke findin' her?" The underling asked.

"No, it is not important, she is only an opportunistic street slut anyhow, I can get another girlie if I want to; did that last shipment arrive on time?"

"Yes Mister Q, Jonno delivered it to the cutting room this morning."

"Have a small quantity delivered home here by tonight, Bling!"

"Yes Mister Q."

As Bling left, Olly got to surmising, he really did want another go at that spirited bitch; he could see for himself that underneath all of her paint she really was a good looker.

'Got to have another go with her.' He thought to himself. Olly summoned his man servant.

"Yes Mister Q?" His servant asked when he arrived, very subserviently.

"When Slugger is off the 'phone, send him in!"

The man servant bowed as he left.

"You wanted me Mister Q?" Slugger asked as he hurried into Olly's presence.

"Friday evening see if you can pick up that girlie at the Casino!"

"Will do, she may not be there you know."

"I think she will, she evidently likes the better clientele there, it is worth a try anyway." Olly had a smug expression on his oily face.

Slugger was waiting with the doorman at the casino the next Friday evening, they both looked expectantly at each passing lady hoping Beryl would put in an appearance. Both were disappointed, Beryl was nowhere to be seen.

"Do you think she may have got in through the gaming section?"

Slugger asked the doorman.

"No, it's not possible for her to do that, there is a doorman on the entry into the elite part of the casino; I doubt that anyone could slip past security. I guess she is just not going to put in an appearance."

"Reckon I'd better look in a few of the eateries in case she got in somehow. Slugger was well known to the doorman through Olly Quinton; he entered.

Slugger tried three cafe's before he came across Beryl, she was dining with a patron of the casino and was evidently in a happy state of mind. Slugger bided his time, he could wait an hour or two if necessary; this it would seem was one of those necessities.

His chance came as Beryl headed for the ladies rest room, he waited until she left and was returning to her table. Taking her by the elbow Slugger made for the exit. Beryl resisted.

"Hey! Let me go, I have a date waiting for me!" She feebly attempted to go.

"Your date is with me, remember - we are going to see Mister Q - he needs you again. Now come quietly and do not cause a disturbance or you may regret it as I have it in

121

my power to mark you!" Slugger quickly ushered her out and away.

"I have no desire to service Olly as I have a higher quality client now!"

Beryl's argument fell upon deaf ears as she was hustled away from the venue's car parking facility and became quite anxious as she beheld the revolver upon her abductor's knee; aimed at her.

They arrived at the most opulent home of Olly Quinton and as Slugger got out and went around to her side to open the door, Beryl noticed that he left the keys in the car so she quickly slipped into the driver's seat and sped away with Slugger vainly attempting to cling to the vehicle. As it gathered speed he was forced to let go and rolled upon the gravel surface, he arose and shook a fist at his stolen vehicle before dusting himself down. Beryl smiled grimly to herself as she travelled back to the metropolis, realising that she had better ditch the limousine somewhere away from her usual haunts, because for sure Olly and his underlings would seek her with malice now.

Beryl abandoned the vehicle near a taxi rank and took a cab back to the casino, hoping upon hope that Jerry would still be there. She now relied upon him to get her to a safe haven from Olly and his men, the memory of Slugger and his pistol was still very firmly in her mind. As she was dropped off near the parking area of the casino, Beryl made her way to where she remembered that Jerry parked his car. Thankfully she gasped in relief when she saw that it was still awaiting it's owner; she patiently waited beside it hoping that Jerry would soon come for his vehicle. Nor had she long to wait.

Jerry had looked to the ladies rest room many times expecting momentarily that Beryl would emerge, he did not know that Beryl had been escorted away earlier, he had been engrossed with his wine and those about that were his acquaintances. Worried that Beryl was over long in coming, Jerry summoned the waitress and asked would she see if perhaps Beryl was ailing. The waitress returned to report that the rest room was vacant. Jerry thanked her and frowned that such a thing could be, perhaps it was too daunting upon Beryl to accept the great change that would be Beryl's lot if she were to bow to his wishes and try to alter her lifestyle; it must have seemed too much for her to cope with and Beryl had changed her mind. Jerry finished his wine and left the cafe' to make his way home, very disappointed that she had just up and left him. Surprise - surprise, as he was approaching his vehicle there she was awaiting him.

"I thought that I had lost you, why did you leave without letting me know Beryl; if you wished to go early I would have accompanied you?" He smiled.

"Let us go quickly and I will explain!" Beryl urgently pleaded. "Quickly!"

Jerry opened the door for her then hurriedly got behind the wheel and they sped away. He looked at her with raised eyebrows, seeking an answer.

"I got taken away forcibly by a thug - he - he pointed a gun at me and took me to his master, when he alighted to open the door for me I quickly slipped into the driver's seat and stole his car; I left it at a taxi rank and hurried here. I only just arrived when you came - thankfully - please, you have to get me away from the casino to a safe place; they will kill me for nicking off on them especially now that I pinched their limousine!" Beryl had the fear of death in her gaze as she pleaded with Jerry.

"You are not kidding I can see that you are terrified, who are these people - are they the same ones who took you before?" Jerry worried.

"Yes, the same, Olly is the boss's name, I believe he is just a fat pig of a man who runs a slimy business of some sort; he owns a couple of strong arm boys to do his dirty work for him. He frightens me, do you have a safe place that I can go to, if he catches me again he will mark me for sure!" Beryl trembled.

"Do you have anything extremely dear to you at your lodgings?"

"At my home I do but nobody knows where that is, I have kept my private place to myself as a refuge, I have photographs of my parents and personal stuff there; all my clothes - going out clothes that is - not these glamour rags I use for my profession. Why?" Beryl guardedly asked.

Jerry put her at ease as he could see she was still very guarded for her safety.

"We have to leave everything behind that is not important to you, clothes can be easily replaced - photographs cannot - if your really personal things are safe where they are we can leave them be for the present. I am going to outfit you as befitting a lady so your professional rubbish can be forgotten about, you will no longer have any use for it. Where we are going now is to my country mansion, it is about fifty kilometres away and is very remote so far as townships go; it is just outside a lovely little country township called Belgrave. You will be safe there and I am well-known to the locals." Jerry was happy.

Beryl heaved a sigh of relief, at least for a while she could relax.

"Is Belgrave where you live?"

"Not all the time, I have a large home in Toorak when I am working but I am not at the office very often these days; I have very efficient staff and they keep the concerns all viable. No use having a dog and barking yourself!"

"Huh?" Beryl turned troubled eyes towards him.

Jerry could see that the analogy was not understood by Beryl, he elaborated.

"When one has businesses all over then one has to rely on staff to do the thinking for you, I am involved in multiple enterprises which are becoming world-wide and therefore many people work for me; it is useless for me to become involved in the majority of my companies when I have staff being paid to do it for me!" His benevolent smile was infectious.

Beryl smiled too. Shaking her head in wonder she queried.

"What sort of businesses are you running?"

"Well I started out in Antiques but that business flourished so well that I began dabbling in imports and that took off too, so of course I had to get extra staff and then managers for that staff and it just blossomed from there. Now it is so large that I am more or less redundant so far as managing the businesses go; I mostly am only needed to pave the direction in which I wish them to go. Board meetings and the like!" Jerry nodded contentedly to himself.

Beryl looked in amazement at her companion, it was only just beginning to permeate her mind that this Jerry was much more than merely a pick-up that happened to meet her in a posh suburb; this man was an important nabob of society. She was dumbfounded that he had taken such a fancy to her. Beryl, a common 'street-girl' was now favoured by this champion of society, a man who could buy the favours of more ladies of fashion, than those that strutted the red carpets of glamour emporiums set by film studios or charity concerns. Beryl was now becoming over-awed by the stroke of good fortune into which she had stumbled.

"Are you - are you sure that you want to take the risk of trying to make a lady out of me? I am beginning to take fright at the enormity of what is about to happen!" Beryl began to tremble, Jerry could see that it was boiling inside of her. He pulled the motor into a quiet little nook under the hillside that they were passing at the time and he attempted to settle her down.

"Now do not let this matter get to you Beryl, sure I do live in high society and I know that it seems very daunting to you but it will not be all that hard for you to cope you know; I and my people at my mansion will guide you very gently so that you can settle in all right. Just be patient and see what I have at Belgrave, they are really nice people and will do as I direct; you need not worry."

Beryl's head was swimming, it all seemed so unreal to her, for sure her luck had changed and this man Jerry Thorn-dyke, definitely had taken a huge liking to her - a 'street-girl' - a prostitute; she was now so overwhelmed that she became speechless. As they purred along the small highway towards Belgrave, the silence of his companion got to Jerry, he again tried to put her at ease.

"The Simpson's are my caretakers at the country mansion, you will get to like them; Missus Simpson was my nanny when I was but a child. She is my house keeper - come servant-maid now. Mister Simpson has been our chauffeur since they got married and the pair of them have been in the family employ all of their married lives. They are nice people and very true to the family - well - to my parents when they were here, they are semi-retired now but they still are very true to me; they were a little reticent about my ex wife though! It is a strange thing that, you know, they could never get over me marrying her, they did not get on too well with her - we nearly lost them one time because of her. Nanny was right as usual, she is very perceptive and fiercely looks to my best interests; if you trust her implicitly and be guided by her, life will be pleasant for you; she is a stalwart friend as is James - her husband." Jerry smiled at the worried girl beside him.

"Gee! What if she turns her nose up at a common street girl like me? She sounds as if she could very well be a bit uppity with such a common person as I will be to her!" Beryl asked with foreboding.

"Now don't be getting your nickers in a knot over Missus Simpson, she will honour my decision and you will be treated with dignity I can promise you, treat her with respect and she will respect you equally. Here we are now, just be a little subservient and always be polite."

The motor passed a pair of portals that were very impressive and began the journey along the avenue of trees leading to a round-a-bout in front of the most imposing mansion. Two people appeared at the door of the mansion to welcome the visitors.

"How did they know we were coming?" Beryl asked.
"The house is equipped with sensors everywhere, when we entered through the front gates a signal inside the house activated to let them know that there were visitors." Jerry enlightened Beryl.

As his vehicle pulled in front of the mansion near the verandah, Mister Simpson dutifully attended the door of Jerry's car. A happy smile greeted them.
"Good evening Sir, welcome home!" He allowed Jerry to alight and then attended Beryl's side of the vehicle and did a like service for her.
"Good evening Miss, follow me please."
Beryl sedately followed and the party entered the imposing mansion.
"This lady is Beryl, she will be my guest for a couple of weeks or so!"
Jerry introduced all and they settled into the lounge room for drinks and a chat.

When James had gone about his duties which included driving the motor to its garage, and they were about to sample the drinks; Missus Simpson hovered nearby awaiting instructions.

"I am so sorry Missus Simpson for not announcing our arrival but it was decided at short notice and it was urgent, so we regrettably had very little time to inform you that we were coming. My lady friend will need some of your most valuable advice upon etiquette and the finer points of becoming a lady that will be befitting her station in our lifestyle. I am going to rely heavily upon you Missus Simpson to give Beryl the tutor-age that she needs; do you think you can manage this for me?"

"Of course Sir, it will be my pleasure, my word it is so nice to see that you have not forgotten us Sir; it must be six months since you last were here you know. I am afraid that the cupboard is a little bare at the moment Sir, I will have to restock tomorrow - I beg your pardon Mister Thorn-dyke - we were taken by surprise at your sudden appearance!" She appeared a little flustered.

"Not to worry at all, it is my fault entirely, now don't you go getting yourself in all of a dither; there is no hurry and we have a couple of weeks to let our hair down and relax. My word but the last couple of months have been quite a worry for me so now it is time for us to relax."

Jerry looked at Beryl, she was rather quiet.

"Now Beryl, remember what we spoke about on the way here, trust Missus Simpson implicitly as I always have because she knows what will be needed for your grooming, her sense of taste is impeccable and her experience over the years has proven her suitability for the job at hand. Perhaps it would be most appreciated if perchance tomorrow, before the supplies are catered for that Missus Simpson should have you properly clothed." He glanced at the maid. Missus Simpson agreed that it could be the best arrangement.

"Would you kindly show Beryl to her quarters and prepare a bath for her?"

"This way Miss." They departed leaving Jerry to contentedly finish his drink.

The next day, while Jerry lazed about the mansion renewing his memories of it and the surrounds, Missus Simpson dutifully went about her duties regarding the purchase of a new wardrobe for the guest. Accompanied by Beryl and chauffeured by her husband James, they attended the local shops.

Although the local shops were a good few kilometres away, it was barely able to be called a township. There were however, ample establishments available to consummate their needs. As Jerry Thorn-dyke was well known to the local business people and his followers too, were equally well known; there were no worries regarding billing all purchases to the mansion.

After the morning shopping spree they returned to the mansion and Missus Simpson spent an hour or so in acquainting Beryl with a few necessary, in fact, urgent, tips on decency in dress and manners. This at first embarrassed the younger lady as she had no idea at all that she was doing anything wrong.

"Please do not be offended Miss, as the Master requested that you be properly groomed in the ways of high society. Mister Thorn-dyke expressly urged that you be properly tutored, so as to 'fit in' with the other ladies at the many social occasions at which you will be expected to attend!"

Missus Simpson gently chided and informed. Beryl smiled and quietly nodded her understanding.

"Thank you Missus Simpson, but all of this business is so strange to me and I feel that I may goof things up inadvertently. After all I was not born to be a lady you know - my upbringing was of a very poor nature. Jerry is taking a huge risk with me - I - I would hate to embarrass him at one of these hoy-polloy gigs!" Beryl had nervous misgivings that she would slip up.

"Just relax and enjoy all of this, I do understand more of your background than I have been informed about, years of pandering to the likes of spoiled children have given me a great insight into the real world. Your past will be forgotten about and never mentioned, providing of course, that you remain true to Mister Thorn-dyke. I and my staff will be true to you as we are to the master; so please be a good girl and pander to our wishes - it will benefit you admirably you know!"

"Yes, I realise that you are all trying to help me, it is a very great shift for me though!" Beryl pleaded. "Missus Simpson, please do let me know if I do step on some toes though - would you? I will be ever so grateful."

"Of course dear, that is my job. Now you just retire to your room and relax a while, I shall summons you for luncheon. Cheers dear, chin up!"

Missus Simpson flounced away merrily.

There was a light tap on her door, Beryl rose from the most comfortable bed upon which she had been resting and opened the door. Jerry was standing there.

"Well, is the room suitable for you?" He asked.

"Oh yes, won't you come in and talk, I have ever so many questions."

He followed her into the room and Beryl again rested upon the bed.

"I am now totally convinced that you are genuine in your resolve to make a lady out of me, I promise you that I will give it my best shot. You will forgive me if I do stuff it up; I will do everything in my power to be true to you as you are the only person in my life that has shown a little charity to me! I - I am overwhelmed that this sort of thing could happen to me, no one has ever before trusted me as you have!" Beryl let a tear run down her cheek. "I can't help it - the servants are so nice and Missus Simpson is such a dear - I am unable to stop the tears; sorry!" Beryl broke down completely and sought her tissue.

"That's it, you have a good cry here in your own private quarters, it will do you good. I will come and get you to escort you to the table when the dinner gong sounds. Try and be a little composed when I come for you, it will just be a private dinner for the two of us so do not panic; it is only like dining at home with your folks. You will not have to pretty yourself up at all."

Jerry smiled comfortingly to reassure her and quietly left.

The gong quietly reverberated throughout the fifteen room mansion and as Jerry had said he would, he was at her door as she opened it; taking Beryl by the arm he escorted her to the prepared table that would become their regular habit. It surprised the guest as she had never before witnessed such a sight. A vase of flowers from the ample gardens in a decorative vase, was placed at the centre of the spread with so much cutlery and many condiments spread about; with coloured serviettes and even bonbons. Beryl was speechless at the sight.

"If you would be seated Miss." James attended her chair and saw that she was settled comfortably. Jerry sat in the chair opposite and Missus Simpson entered the room with a tray upon which were two serves of soup.

"I do hope you enjoy celery soup Miss."

The maid said as she laid them down.

"My word I think I would enjoy plain water on this table!" Beryl gushed.

"I shall bring the venison in for you to carve Sir."

"Oh! I think it would be best if you carve it in the kitchen Missus Simpson, it may be a little too soon for Beryl to experience a formal dinner yet."

"As you wish Sir!" They were left to privately enjoy the soup.

The soup was enjoyed and the main course was then placed for each of them and they were left to themselves again, Jerry spoke with an engulfing smile.

"What do you think Beryl, is lunching in this sort of atmosphere too much for you or do you find it a bit oppressive?"

"This is most certainly very new to me but do you know what? I think I could become really used to it - I am not sure about hoards of people though!"

"Do not worry overly on that matter Beryl, most of our meals are just like this; it is only upon occasions that we have guests and they are just normal people like we are. Sometimes I have important guests to dinner with us but they are just like those in any of the eateries in town, or at the casino. Well to do folk are really not as pompous as you may imagine them to be, business people and the like but they only come once or twice a week; you will enjoy their company and you will blend in nicely if you take the advice of Missus Simpson." Jerry was at pains to put Beryl at her ease.

After they had dined and were relaxing in the lounge to let the meal settle, Beryl confided in Jerry very quietly.

"I don't think that overbearing Mister Q will find me here, I feel very safe with you Jerry, there is no way he could find me here is there?"

"Not at all, and you are very safe here because Missus Simpson has a daughter and she and her husband live in a house about a kilometre away. She is a black belt in Karate and her husband is a second Dan black belt. They run a Karate School not far from here, more in the township. The house is on my property and they act as caretaker - security for me when we have guests here for some of the social functions that my businesses require at times. The house is directly connected to my mansion and they are at my beck and call - they live rent-free so they are very dedicated to me!" He nodded in confirmation.

Beryl looked her amazement at Jerry.

"You keep surprising me Jerry, when I met you I just thought you were a very affluent business man - but gosh - you are more than that, you er, you are a mine of surprises. Where does it all stop?" Beryl was flabbergasted.

"Ah! Don't let it get to you, there is still a lot for you to understand yet; I saw something in you Beryl underneath all of that flouncy stuff you were wearing, there was a lady. In my business one has to be a good judge of character and I fancied that you could be made into that lady. I trust my judgement and I know that given a chance, you could emerge from the mire. Please give yourself a chance to prove me correct, you honestly will Beryl; won't you?" His caring look at her made her heart beat a little faster.

"Yes Jerry, I most certainly will and with Missus Simpson to guide me I know that things are going to work out for the better for me. Better for us!"

Jerry arose and walked around the table to Beryl's side, he gently kissed her cheek..

"That's the girl, do you think that we could become a loving couple, I really do like you you know Beryl and if you become a real lady; there is a mansion here for you to live in and servants to wait on you - it all depends upon how well you and I mould as a couple. Please help me make it work!"

Chapter Three

Mister Q was chatting with his number one man, Slugger, they were in the lounge room and Olly was sipping his bubbly.

"So there is no sign of that little tart I had here that evening?" He asked.

"No Mister Q, she has not been seen since she nicked off with my limo - Lucky the coppers rang to let me know where it was - damn her!"

"Ahh! We'll catch up with her sometime, I can get another girlie when I need one. Now, I have to meet my business partners on Thursday and they will be wondering if I can fulfil the requirement of our most recent shipment; have you had the 'all clear' on that one yet?" He eyed his second-in-command.

"Yes Sir Mister Q, it is finalised and ready for them to collect!"

"Good, see that there are no slip-ups and keep things as low key as possible. We haven't got the Feds on our tails yet but we must be wary of them. My connections in the Force reckon I am still in the clear but you never know when one or another of my tip-offs will be tempted. This latest one is of a very high standard and I will lose a fortune if it goes astray; got that!"

"Yes Sir Mister Q, I will check everything thoroughly. I will make certain that the pick up is the legitimate one, it is usually Morton and he's a mate of mine." Slugger confirmed.

"Oh! Have Bling attend me, I have some business calls to make!"

Slugger nodded as he made his exit to consummate his orders.

Bling quietly sidled up beside Olly and in hand he had the extension telephone; it was offered to Mister Q. Olly took his personal and very private diary from his person and ruffled through the pages.

"Mister Hughes, Olly here, your next shipment is ready; have your man at the pick-up point at nine thirty on Tuesday. Remember, he has five minutes to collect as my men have instructions to return with the shipment if it is not a slick pick-up. I take no chances of it going astray!" Olly hung up.

The telephone rang immediately.

"Olly!" He answered, thinking the call was being returned.

"Ah! Mister Q - Tomas. There is another shipment coming and it is a big one - er - are you up to it? My connections inform me that it is due on the sixth, it must be clear of the airport immediately it arrives. I demand a very slick operation with no stuff-ups and immediate settlement. Is that clear?"

Olly agreed and made the necessary arrangements. He heaved a satisfied grunt and thought of the profits that could be looked forwards to when everything was accomplished. This was a greater risk than previous cargoes but the rewards would make it worth while. His satisfied smirk was premature.

Detective John Mann from the Special Branch knocked and entered the office of his superior at the busy central office of the Phoenix Squad. The man behind the desk was a very heavily built chap with a worried frown upon his features, features that could become very stern with any person that interrupted his concentration.

"Yes Mann, what is the urgency?" He asked without looking up.

"An intercepted call from Olly Quinton Sir, from someone he called 'Tomas', I believe he is an importer Sir!" A slip of paper was presented.

"Ah! This looks promising, has it been traced yet?"

"Not completed yet Sir, we are working upon it, the call was from Asia."

"Let me know immediately that you have the connection monitored. This could be the break-through we have been missing. Good work!"

"There is something else Sir, Olly's prior call was from a local 'phone and it would appear that this was from a 'buyer'; we are chasing that one up too Sir!"

"Ah! Good, now things are moving - get right back to me when you have the connections properly monitored. I need this information immediately!"

Detective John Mann took his leave.

Super-intendant Hallam Hoskins turned to his immediate assistant in the room with him and very authoritatively ordered the man to attend the radio operator.

"It is most urgent that we follow this lead up with alacrity and be sure that all incoming calls are correctly monitored. This may be the turning point for the collaring of the Mister Bigs of the cartel that has been operating in our area. We must be very alert now for the most insignificant of leads that could give us an inkling into the heart of our problem. I feel that we are on the verge of a break-through, this 'Tomas' may be the head but I want to find out who is the local buyer!"

Sergeant Barry Tench hurried to do as ordered.

Super-intendant Hoskins rang through to his squad room.

"Masterson, I want a 'tail' put on Olly Quentin's head man - er - I think his name is 'Slugger', find out his true name if you can, that should not be hard. We have information that Olly is in something big at the moment and we have to turn the screws a bit. There are to be no slip-ups, this must be kept very low key!"

"Yes Sir!" Sergeant Masterson began the operation.

So it was that when Slugger drove from Olly's premises to do as he was ordered, unbeknown to him, he was 'tailed' everywhere he went.

Back at the mansion, Jerry Thorn-dyke was busy too, his immediate worry was to be sure that Beryl was safe from Olly. To this end he secured the services of his close friend and body guard; Tom Mand. Tom and his wife Jane were both black belt karate instructors having their own business tutoring in and around their country township of Belgrave but their clientele came from afar too. Tom jumped at the call from his benefactor and came immediately he was summoned.

Jerry and Tom were attending a secret meeting within the mansion unknown to Beryl, she was being instructed by Missus Simpson in the art of correct manners for a person of quality as expected in higher society. Jerry and Tom were in a very serious conversation where Jerry stressed the point that this action must be kept away from Beryl. Nothing should disturb her from concentrating upon her duties at hand.

"You see Tom" Jerry stressed. "Beryl is terrified that this Olly person will attempt to get even with her for not acquiescing to his wishes, he is evidently a very powerful man in his own dung-heap. She has quietly confided with me that he has a couple of strong-arm boys in his employ. They have already threatened to cut her of her good looks; these sound like desperadoes of the lowest type. I will need for them to know that she has very good desperadoes of her own to counter them. I know you are quite able to match them in any physical encounter but you have a mental capacity that is far and above their limited capabilities. Is what I ask of you in any way not to your liking, if so I will not hold it against you?" Jerry frowned at Tom.

"No, I have it covered Mister Thorn-dyke, it will be my pleasure to put a crimp in Olly Quinton's schemes, you see, I have a couple of clients that have fallen victim to his henchmen; they came to my school to prepare themselves from his toughs. He is known to the underworld of dealing in

137

drugs, I have no proof of this but my clients tell me he is very involved; a man of absolutely no principals at all"

"Really? Gee I never realised just what Beryl had gotten herself mixed up with. Will that make any difference to my employing you for this task?"

"Not at all, I rather like the idea of becoming involved for my client's sakes, it may even be of use to the authorities if perchance I do get to know of their plans through the agency of the toughs!" Tom had his turn at a satisfied grin.

"Gee! I do hope that this business is not going to get out of hand, perhaps getting the authorities involved may be to our advantage but it is putting you and yours at a very great risk. I will make enquiries at my board meetings and see if anyone knows of this Olly - er - Quinton, is it?" Jerry was quite worried for Tom.

"That may be a good idea as you too are an importer, perhaps some of your contacts have been queried about the possibilities of importing his merchandise?"

"I have not heard of any such goings on, however my staff may have been approached - that is a good point - thanks for warning me Tom. Are you quite sure that it is not going to cause you any trouble" Jerry's real concern made Tom smile.

"No Sir Mister Thorn-dyke, I am actually looking forwards to becoming involved. In a way I do hope that we do get some solid proof that Olly is importing drugs, because I would like to work with the police on this matter and stop this craze for abuse of our children. These people do not care about the damage they are doing to our kids - all they want is to make money - the greedy bas- er- excuse me Sir; greedy damn bloodsuckers. I would love to be able to stamp them out!"

This clandestine meeting gave Jerry cause for some deep thinking. Tom went back to his wife to brief her upon the outcome of his meeting with 'The Boss' as they referred to Jerry, and set plans in motion for further enquiries of Olly Quinton. Jerry was engulfed in his own worries for Beryl's safety. If this Olly was a successful businessman - albeit a crooked one - then it were a possibility that he could have personnel in high places; like politicians or even corrupt members of the police force. Jerry would have to step carefully, he had friends himself in high places such as he thought Olly may have but he did not think any of his contacts were corrupt. That might just be his advantage over Olly.

Meanwhile Slugger was consummating his commitments for Olly and was at an address in the suburbs, it was a rather posh-looking business house that had nothing to do with drugs or contraband from its outside looks. However, clandestinely, it was a hive of hidden underworld activity. The person who opened the door just looked at whom the caller was and admitted him entry. Not a word was spoken. Slugger went through one of the doors leading to the rear of the premises, knocked and entered. A sleasy-looking tough nodded him past and Slugger spoke abruptly to the smartly dressed man in the high arm chair.

"Mister Hughes, I have your latest shipment aboard; where do you want it delivered?" Slugger was the regular interchange.

Gruen Hughes smiled.

"Would you deliver it to my Clifton Hill warehouse? This chit will be paid on confirmation that all is in order!"

He wrote a note and tore it off the pad, then gave it to Slugger. That person accepted the chit and went back to his vehicle. He drove to the Clifton Hill address, waited for the check up, then when it was all clear, he received a small satchel of payment for the goods. His vehicle only got to the next intersection when flashing blue lights on a police car blocked his path. The satchel was confiscated and Slugger was read his rights and taken to the police station. At the same time another three police cars were at the warehouse and three men were arrested there too.

Olly Quinton was ropeable, he had just hung up his telephone and was told of the arrests. He picked up a vase and threw it at the wall, swearing blue murder about his losses and the fact of his main man Slugger being apprehended.

"Bugger the bloody cops and their flaming interference. How the hell did they know Slugger was carrying my bloody merchandise? By crikey I'll find the leak and then someone will get a pair of concrete boots!" He went back to his desk and slammed a fist into it.

"They must have me bugged, how the bloody hell did they get on to my shipment? I know I can trust Slugger - and he does not squeal - who did, dammit?"

Having been arrested for the possession of a very large sum of money and also of delivering a great quantity of illicit drugs, as he had been followed by the authorities; Slugger was taken into custody. At his appearance before a magistrate he was given the benefit of the doubt when he appealed that he was only obeying his master's instructions and as a carrier; he was the innocent party. The magistrate allowed Slugger bail until his next appearance.

"Damn the rotten police, they must have had you 'tailed', so now they are aware of my home, one of my outlets (which they have shut down) and arrested three of my clients. Brewster should get you off when your trial comes up but I doubt if he will be able to help my clients. Stuff the bloody coppers! Hell, I have lost thousands now that they have confiscated my dough and the rotten drugs as well. I only hope that they don't get on to this next lot that is coming in - they may have my 'phone line bugged - I had better ring Tomas and change the arrivals at the airport. I'll do it from outside, I have some private contacts that I can ring him from. Slugger, you had better stay low for a bit; I am going to arrange this myself." Olly concluded.

Meanwhile Tom had visited his clients and got some valuable information from them regarding who and where this 'Olly Quinton was. To this end he made a call at the Police headquarters. Tom asked to see Sergeant Barry Tench, an old friend.

"G'day Tom. What brings you here, got a parking ticket - I am not able to help you with it - regulations you know; or is it something else?" Barry asked.

"No, it is something else and I may be able to help you!" Tom grinned.

"Oh that sounds interesting, something else eh? Has it to do with your field - you know - Karate, I had one of your clients in the other day; he wanted to know if he would be held responsible for breaking an arse hole's neck! I think he was only kidding but he was serious about his rights."

"No Tom, but it could have some connections, do you know of an Olly Quinton?"

Barry gave Tom a cautious worried look.

"Yes?"

"You know my Boss, Jerry Thorn-dyke, well he has a friend that has been getting bothered by Olly and has recruited me to look into the matter. I was wondering if perchance I may get a little legal backing in case things get out of hand. Can you help?" Tom had a worried look upon his face.

"Olly Quinton eh Crikey, you pick some beauts don't you? I think you had better speak to the big man. Follow me!"

He led the way. Knocking upon a door he ushered Tom into an office.

"Superintendent, this is Tom Mand, he has a Karate School in the country and needs our help, it concerns Olly Quinton!" Barry introduced them.

"Olly Quinton eh! How does it concern Olly, has this to do with an illicit transaction?" Hallam Hoskins asked.

"No Sir, not as yet, I may need some sort of legal guarantee that is why I have come here Sir; I am a friend of Barry and I came to him for advice. Straight away he thought it better to bring me to you, I have been recruited by my Master to protect one of his clients from this Olly; he is a quite powerful person in his field Sir - so I am informed - and I deemed it better to have the authorities on my side."

"A very good point - er - do you have any concrete proof of any of Olly's doings? We are investigating him at the present so anything you may have could be important to us!" Inspector Hallam mused.

"No Sir, not as yet but I do have clients that are being worried by his thugs and things may become a little sticky as I make enquiries Sir. I want to be within the law in what decisions I may be forced into." Tom worried.

"You may have just come to a sensible conclusion Mister Mand, if at all you are getting mixed up in the affairs of this Olly Quinton you certainly will need to be backed up by the law. Now for a start we do not want any outside interference in our activities. We have only just made inroads into his network and will not tolerate some do-gooder interfering with our plans - got that? We have under cover agents spread all over and you might just bungle your way into our infrastructure!"

He gave Tom a blithering stare.

"That is the reason that I demand your co-operation Sir, I have no intention of stepping on your toes or those of your agents. As a private citizen I just wish to be of assistance but I also have responsibilities to my clients, I must be seen to be doing my duties Sir!" Tom was adamant.

"Well of course we cannot stop you from doing what a normal being is entitled to do - however - we can forbid your interference into police matters. Now let me see, this may be to our advantage to have an outsider who is not connected to the law in any way on our side. Just give me a moment to mull this over will you?"

Superintendent Hoskins conferred with his associates quietly aside from Tom.

After having waited ten or so minutes, Superintendent Hoskins returned and with him was a very stern looking man of apparent great importance.

"This is Captain Smerdon, co-ordinator of the Phoenix Squad, who wishes to speak with you Mister Mand." Superintendent Hoskins introduced them.

"You are an instructor of Karate?" The Captain asked.

"Yes Sir, I run the Mand Karate School just out of Belgrave with my wife - she is also a Martial Arts Master, Sir!"

"And you have been recruited by your employer to look into the activities of this Olly Quentin - er - what activities exactly?" The Captain asked.

"Stand over activities Sir! You see Mister Jerry Thorn-dyke has a lady friend who is being threatened by Olly Quentin's thugs - they have already threatened to scar her good looks and are chasing around to find her - so I have been asked to look to her safety." Tom Mand explained.

"I see, er, what action did you have in mind?"

"I have not come to any sort of action at the moment Sir, I deemed it best to see what my legal rights were first; so I sought advice from my friend Sergeant Barry Tench, he recommended I speak to Detective Mann!"

Captain Smerdon rubbed his chin as he cogitated upon this matter. Coming to a conclusion, the Captain addressed this latest stranger to their enquiries regarding Olly Quinton.

"Mister Mand, are you willing to act as an undercover agent for us in the apprehension of some very 'heavy' no-goods that are threatening our children with drugs? You may have to be sworn in as an agent for us after we have checked out your suitability. It is most important that we scrutinise your past so that there can be no hiccups to impair your value to our cause, we are urgently needing a suitable person that has absolutely no connections to law enforcement - at least so far as the underworld is concerned - a 'sleeping' agent if you will. Are you willing to be that person?" The beetling stare was fastened upon this surprised individual.

"But I am not trained in law enforcement – I am only a specialist in Martial Arts - it would take years to have me ready for that Sir, the immediate problem is more important to my employer; time is of the essence you know." Tom worried.

"You will not be needed to enforce the law, all we will want from you is co-operation and an insight into what knowledge you can gain, in your quest for the safety of your client. You see Mister Mand, any only slight contact from an outside source such as you will be when you have difficulties with this mob; may give us a pointer into Olly Quentin's criminal activities. It is most important that we have actual and real proof that he is stepping outside the law. You may just be the one to gain this intelligence even though it may not be important to you - it could be most important to us! Where he is and at what time, who is with him or working for him - such minor details could bring him down with any unlawful activities. Do you understand the very great boon to us that you may be?" Captain Smerdon urged.

Tom frowned at the Captain, nodding to himself. With chin high he agreed.

"Yes Sir, I am at your service; what needs to be done now?"

"For the time being just go about your every day duties while we check your background, I am sure that it will prove you capable; then when we have clearance of your suitability - we will be in contact. Possibly a week or two, Detective Mann will notify you - do what you have to for the time being and thank you for doing your civic duty."

Tom was dismissed and went home somewhat relieved for his legal backing.

Chapter Four

Meanwhile Beryl was being given a crash course in good manners that were a requirement for a lady of quality in high society circles. Her clothing had changed greatly, gone were the gaudy street-girl rags that were once upon her very shapely body, with proper grooming and a more beneficial hair-do and professional make-up Beryl; had the outer appearance of a lady. It was the inner traits of a sordid life style that was in urgent need of transformation. Beryl, upon looking at the reflection in her full length mirror, realised that her outside appearance was astonishing in its total change for her. She knew deep down that looks alone does not make one a lady - a change must also be applied to her character - Beryl must learn all she could about the ways of a lady of substance. This was her chance, her great chance, she had a gentleman for an escort who was rich and important in society; who has shown that he really cares for her deeply. That man had shown that he was prepared to bend over backwards for her in the quest to make her a lady of refinement. Beryl was determined to do her utmost to bring his dreams to a reality. To get out of the rat-race that she had been born into and lead a truly admirable life-style, she would strive her hardest to do what was expected of her. Jerry was really a remarkable young man, well reasonably young, and Beryl could hardly believe that he had taken such a liking to her; she would do her utmost in succumbing to his wishes.

Jerry had been required to attend his business matters as a matter of urgency since becoming involved with his new lady. Missus Simpson was a very accomplished person of true integrity and he knew that Beryl was in the best of care with her attending to Beryl's needs. So Jerry was back to steering his business as he wished it to progress and to thrive, it really could be directed without him as his business managers were top notch men of integrity, however Jerry would prefer that he was seen to be still in control of things and was keeping an eye upon his business ventures. When these matters were dealt with, Jerry was back at his mansion near Belgrave. As usual he was welcomed back with enthusiasm by his staff.

Missus Simpson and her husband James, dutifully were at hand to greet him and to await instructions when Jerry arrived with a huge smile.

"Time to relax Sir, shall I garage your vehicle or do you wish it to be available immediately?"

"Yes you can put it away for the day James - er - Missus Simpson, a nice glass of red would be welcome thank you; I shall be in the lounge. Would you ask Beryl to pop down please?"

He breezed past and went to put his feet up on the pouffe.

As Missus Simpson was pouring his wine and before she could summon Beryl; that lady walked down the staircase.

"I heard the chimes to announce a visitor and glanced out to see whom it was, I was so pleased to see you had returned. May I join you?" Beryl asked.

"Of course, my word your vocabulary has progressed very well Beryl, it is so gratifying that you have heeded the tutorage of Missus Simpson. I notice too, that your deportment as you descended the staircase, is most appropriate for a lady of some substance. What a remarkable transformation you are demonstrating and I am so very pleased that you have acquiesced to my urging that you do so. Please sit with me so that I may appreciate your charms and we can catch up with our social life."

Jerry attended a chair for her before James could do it, he bowed and stood aside.

"Thank you." She sweetly murmured.

James poured a Julep for her as that is what she preferred.

"Oh! I see that you really are becoming a lady of good taste!"

Jerry smiled as he witnessed this somewhat different behaviour of Beryl's.

"Yes, Missus Simpson introduced me to a Julep, I had never tasted one before and as she recommended it as a more appropriate drink for a lady - well - it is rather a nice change for me." Beryl had a gleam in her eyes that was foreign to Jerry.

"So you can see as I predicted, Missus Simpson knows exactly what is in your best interests - do you recall that I recommended that you properly heed her very good taste?" Jerry too, had a gleam in his smiling eyes that beheld her beauty.

"Yes I will always remember that, I has made me think very deeply of the chance that you have afforded me; I will be ever grateful of that!"

Jerry changed the subject for he could see the matter was becoming a problem if he made Beryl feel obliged to fawn upon him.

"I have spoken to Tom - he is my protector - when I have need of a body-guard, and he is aware of Olly Quinton and his strong arm boys. Tom runs a Karate School with his wife and they are both black belts, in fact a couple of his clients are also being bothered by this Olly's thugs. Tom is going to look into it for us and you should be free of Olly from now on - does that make you feel safer?"

"Oh yes, but I always feel safe when I am with you Jerry; there should be no problems with him way out here anyway." Beryl smiled happily.

"No, I believe he is not aware that you have left the metropolis. You should not have any fear of him interfering with you at this safe haven. Is everything here to your liking Beryl? I would not wish you to be unhappy with your new lifestyle, I know that you are trying very hard to fit in as it were and I thank you for that. It is not too restrictive is it?"

"Ooh - it is gorgeous - I am more than happy to be away from the big smoke and into the country air, it is so clean and refreshing in the countryside; I am so happy here. Especially so as you have given me Missus Simpson - she is such a dear - and her tutor-age is so refreshing. I do not believe even a school mistress could teach me so well as Missus Simpson has done."

Beryl looked at Jerry so lovingly that he became a little surprised.

"My word Beryl, you are becoming quite a lady; how flattering!"

"There is one thing though." Beryl noted.

"Yes?" Jerry queried.

"Boredom! I have nothing to interest me when Missus Simpson goes about her duties, I need an interest of some sort - you see - I am out of my comfort zone and cannot even repair to my home comforts here. I need to be doing something, I do not knit and there is no need for me to solicit strangers any more; I need a hobby or some kind of work to keep me occupied." Beryl raised her eyebrows in query.

"Yes, we must give you some kind of occupation that will keep you interested when I am at work; that is a good point. You mentioned that you have a retreat in the city proper; with your most cherished personal belongings. What say I have James drive you there and you can pick them up, just get what is really necessary - leave anything else - and make a full move up here? Only if you are comfortable living here with me, if the premises you have as your own private retreat is yours, well you can rent it out; otherwise let it go to someone else."

"The place was left to me by my parents when they passed, I just rented a room to work from. You see, I needed to keep my own house private from my clients in case I was followed home. In the calling I had it was most appropriate as the majority of my clients were somewhat of a motley lot and they could not be trusted. I had to be aware of a mugging on my way home, some of my clients were capable of paying for a service then getting it back -and more - by assault."

"Gosh you were in a predicament with your lifestyle weren't you?"

Jerry had a most concerned and worried look upon his rather handsome features.

Having come to a conclusion regarding Beryl's predicament, it was arranged that James escorted her to her own lodgings to gather her private things such as photographs etcetera, have that house rented out and then she could more comfortably settle in at Jerry's mansion up near Belgrave. They set about this task.

It was a visit to an Estate Agent that brought Beryl undone. Olly Quentin happened to be coming out of a Men's Wear Fashion premises opposite when he stopped to gawk at the well-to-do couple departing the estate agent's. Noting that her escort seemed to be a little old for the lady, he also noticed that she was beautiful and carried herself with great deportment; it gave him to wonder why she would be interested in such an older man. Something was familiar to Olly, he was sure that he had seen the lady before but was at pains to remember where. Then as he ogled it came to him, she was the street girl that he ordered his henchman - Slugger - to bring to him and she absconded with the man's vehicle.

"The bitch!" He exclaimed as he attempted to cross the road so as to accost her. His efforts were in vain as the traffic was against him and allowed the pair to escape him; all unaware that they had been seen by Olly. He tried to remember the license plate of their vehicle, not sure if he could remember it he fumed about the matter.

Olly Quentin was at his own place and speaking with one of his hired hands.

"Get over to Vince and see if you can find out who owns the Bentley of this number plate!" He ordered. The man departed.

Beryl returned to the mansion all unaware of the disturbing affair with Olly Quentin. When James had assisted her into her private quarters with her personal things acquired from her home, Beryl had a meeting with Jerry.

"Having untied yourself from the city, you are now a local and therefore I deem it a good thing if you become involved with the local charities Beryl; what do you think of that for an interest?" Jerry grinned at her.

"Local charities - in what manner do you believe I would be wanted, I mean - I would not know where to start, how would I fit in there?"

"It is easier than you might think Beryl, you see the local charities are forever seeking staff and anyone who can donate their time is always so welcome. Not only would it be an interest for you but you will also make very good friends there, they are not at all a stuffy lot but real down-to-earth people. Their main aim is to help the needy and make a hard life for some, just a little bit easier. You will find that assisting those who need help is a very fulfilling occupation. You can spend as much or as little time as you desire there, they are not a bit picky and are an easy lot to get on with. I do believe that would be better for you to become involved in than just moping about with time on your hands; shall I take you there and you may give it a try?" Jerry beamed.

"Give me a day to think about it, will you Jerry? I am not sure of myself."

Meanwhile Tom was back at his gymnasium consummating his commitments there as usual and it was whilst training the customer who was having trouble with Olly Quentin's thugs, that he was asked if he was making any progress with his enquiries.

"I have just been speaking with my Detective friend about that matter and checked what the legal situation was for me, it is very promising so just bear with me for a few days and I could have the roughnecks off your back. Do not do anything foolish just yet - we have to have things legal and above board!"

"Thanks, I did not want to rush in when I am not ready for combat as yet. How will you tackle this situation with me?" Peter Lofts asked.

"You will not be involved with this at all Peter, I am awaiting word from my Detective friend that I will be legally recruited to assist the police, then I can get things moving - just be patient!" Tom enlightened.

"Wow, that will make a difference won't it?"

"Yes and with Police backing I will have to abide by the law; this is to be kept top secret just between you and I. Is that firmly understood?"

"It sure will be, if you do need assistance am I able to be any help at all?"

Tom smiled and nodded.

"If and when I do need an assistant I will call upon you, just be patient."

Chapter Five

The very next day Beryl attended breakfast with Jerry who was smiling broadly, he asked how did she feel today.

Beryl let a delightful smile enhance her beautiful features as she answered.

"Absolutely wonderful Jerry, you know I had a good think about that proposition you came up with yesterday - and do you know what? I really think that you may have guided me into the right direction - you know, with that suggestion you made regarding doing a little charity work. I believe that would be a very good pastime for me to consider; now how do I go about it?"

Her wide open eyes had a gleam of intrigue about them.

"Ah! I am so pleased to hear that - Missus Simpson is the person you should ask that of - she often gives a hand out herself when I am not here to be catered for - Missus Simpson will guide you to whom you should discus matters with, she will take you and introduce you to the staff there. It should be a wonderful experience for you and you will meet many of the locals; get to know who is about and all of the local gossip etcetera. I think that you will enjoy yourself immensely, the people that run it are lovely folk and they are forever needing assistance. Now do not go overdoing it for a start, gently does it and you can add a little as you get accustomed to what will be required of you, it will be just observing for a start and then when you become more into it; then you will find charity work a wonderful helping pastime."

When next Missus Simpson attended him, Jerry outlined the gist of what was proposed for Beryl to her and it was left in her most capable hands to set Beryl upon her introduction to charity work. Jerry arranged a suitable motor vehicle for Beryl which would make her independent of the restrictions of having to be ferried about by his staff. A most satisfactory event for all as this vehicle - although small - gave her that little bit of freedom which made her feel very comfortable. She blossomed as a lady of substance and her life attained new meaning and direction; hers was becoming a very satisfied lifestyle that did have a purpose. Beryl was blending into high society a little.

Olly Quinton was in a quandary, his business ventures were being undermined and after having come across that bitch of a girl who nicked off with Slugger's vehicle, just a slimy little tart; he was becoming apoplectic. Alright, so she was just a common prostitute but she had pulled a fast one on Olly and he was not of a forgiving nature. His man whom was given the task of checking the registration number on the limousine that the old geezer that accompanied her drove, checked out to be owned by an importer whom he had no knowledge of - this too would have to be checked out! But Olly was no nearer to finding out where the old codger lived. His temper was not abated.

He would bide his time and perchance his man would follow it through and come up with something useful. Olly went about his arrangements with his illegal drug shipments.

Two days later Vince rang Olly, he had managed to find out at the establishment where the limo' in question was registered, that it was a chauffeured vehicle at the service of one Jerry Thorn-dyke; a wealthy Antique Dealer and Importer. Further enquiries gave Olly Quentin to understand that this Jerry Thorn-dyke had an away-from-home retreat in a country township called Belgrave. He set Vince to the task of locating this retreat!

Beryl was duly introduced into charity work at her local shopping centre. The staff welcomed her with open arms as they did with all volunteers, but when it was found that she was a guest of their most ardent supporter; her value to the cause was especially appreciated. Beryl found that life was beginning to blossom with her new interest. She melded into the community as if she had spent her life-time there. This little venture into the wonderful world of assisting others in need, gave her to understand just how many people there were who really needed a boost in life; if at all she had any self-pity for her past it came home to her in reality that her past was as nothing in comparison to many, many others. Beryl had now at last come to the realisation that her own life had indeed blossomed and that she was now in a position to help others - a position to which she had never given any thought to in her past life!

She was mixing well with the staff and as she became a little more comfortable with them, a stranger was pointed out to her; it was Vince who happened to be walking past the shop. Of course he was not known to any one there as he had never been to this township before, it was strange to him. The lady in charge at the time - Vera Collins - nodded towards him as he sauntered by and confided to Beryl.

"See that stranger, he is well-dressed and could be just the type of person who could be coerced into spending some new money into our community; these are the folk that visit and are looking for that odd bargain. We always take note of any stranger who visits because they spend quite often out of curiosity. Although he does seem to be preoccupied, maybe when he has finished the business he came here for he may pop in; one never knows!"

Beryl studied the man out of curiosity herself, thinking that she may learn something from her superior but otherwise took little notice of him. She would have been more alarmed had she known that she herself was his one interest in coming here.

Vince popped in to the local estate agent to make enquiries of this Jerry Thorn- dyke joker. The man behind the desk asked what was his interest in Mister Thorn-dyke.

"Oh! I - er - I just wished to see if he had any land available to purchase, you see, I want to buy a small allotment nearby as a retirement home; a couple of acres would do for me. Does he have a suitable area available please. Perhaps if I called on him we could work something out?"

Vince raised an eyebrow in query.

The estate agent was known to Jerry and the agent was a little suspicious of the stranger - he had odd people come in before, trying to get information about Jerry Thorn-dyke.

"No Sir, Mister Thorn-dyke has his estate and does not wish to butcher it to others, he is a very private person who has good staff to tend his requirements. However, I do have a nice little couple of acres down by the river if you may be interested to have a look at - it is quite reasonably priced."

"Where is Mister Thorn-dyke's home, maybe I could have a talk with him?"

"I am sorry Sir it is our policy not to give out private information to others, it is bad for business you know!"

Without a word Vince about faced and quit the estate agents. He slammed the door as he left. The agent nodded to himself and picked up the telephone. He notified the staff at the mansion there of the stranger who had shown an interest in the Thorn-dyke estate. Once Jerry became aware that there was a stranger showing an interest, he immediately notified Tom Mann. Tom paid a visit to the estate agent.

"G'day Harold, any idea who this chap might be?" Tom opened.

"No Tom, just a blow-in, although by the looks of him and his mannerisms I should guess he is up to no good. He was a rather stocky-looking chap with rather furtive features. I would not say he was a robber though; he was too clean cut for that. More like a seedy business man!"

"Collar and tie?" Tom asked.

"No, open necked shirt and he was wearing a checked brown cardigan and brown trousers, he is slightly grey at the temples!"

"Thanks Harold, he should not be too hard to find if he is still around the township. How long ago did he come in to see you?"

"It would have been about two hours ago I should think, try the local hotel!"

"That is a great idea, he just may be in for lunch!" Tom waved as he left.

The hotel had about a dozen patrons, a few at the bar and the others at the dining tables and at the outside smoking area. One person sitting alone at an isolated table immediately took Tom's attention. That person was unmistakeably the one for whom he was searching. Tom got himself a beverage from the barman and furtively studied the man sitting alone. After fifteen minutes the stranger had dined and drained his glass then arose to leave.

Tom waited until he had gone and then furtively followed the man. He went to a quiet part of the country township where few people could overhear and made a 'phone call, nodding as he received instructions he set off to look for that second-hand shop he had noticed earlier. Tom expectantly awaited his return. Vince casually entered the shop and after picking up a trinket, asked Vera Collins how much was the trinket and had she heard of Mister Thorn-dyke.

"Oh yes, of course." She replied. "Everyone knows of Jerry Thorn-dyke, he is one of our sponsors; he sent our new charity assistant here!"

She pointed out Beryl who was attending to another customer at the moment.

Vince of course had never seen Beryl before, nor did Beryl know Vince, he glanced at her.

"I really need to talk with Jerry, er - could you tell me where his house is by any chance?" Vince offered a note that more than covered the cost of the trinket as he smiled at the lady behind the counter.

"Oh, everyone knows he lives in the mansion just out of town; perhaps Beryl would be the one to speak with - he is not always there you know - he is mostly in the city at his office. I will get Beryl to have a word with you when she has served the customer."

Just then the customer left and Beryl came as she was summoned.

"This gentleman was enquiring after Mister Thorn-dyke, he wishes to speak with him - this is Beryl."

The name 'Beryl' meant nothing to Vince as he did not know her as the 'girlie' that Mister Q was chasing, perhaps she would guide him to her. Beryl openly faced this stranger with a query upon her pretty features, he was not a very pleasant man to look at but that was not her worry, as she treated each customer with a cheery face. Her question was as she would ask everyone.

"How can I be of assistance to you?"

"You are in the confidence of Jerry Thorn-dyke I am told?"

"Yes?" Guardedly.

"I need to have a few words with him, I am told you may be able to help me"

"What do you have to speak with him about?"

"Business deal, where can I find him?" Vince began to look threatening.

Beryl became alarmed as she did not know who this man was but she did recognise his under-world manner.

"Mister Thorn-dyke only speaks to people with an appointment. If you are a genuine businessman you would know that and be invited. I am sorry but I will not give away his personal address!" She turned to attend another customer.

Vince lost his cool and viciously grabbed Beryl by the arm and tugged her out of the shop. Amid screams of anguish by the female staff, who ran to her aid Beryl was forcibly taken around the corner. Vince headed for his auto-mobile.

At the first scream Tom raced to her assistance. Vince was heavily karate-chopped at the neck and fell unconscious to the ground. Beryl was comforted as Tom introduced himself.

"I have been assigned to look out for you, my name is Tom Mand and I am Mister Thorn-dyke's personal bodyguard. Please feel safe and secure when in my company. Are you all right - he did not hurt you?" Tom's look was worried.

"No - just shaken up a little. That man was trying to locate Jerry's home - I refused so then he grabbed me, I was suspicious because he looked like a desperado and so it proved. What do we do about him?" Beryl worried.

"That is all right miss, leave him to me, I will take him to the Police Station and they will attend to him. Shall I take you home?"

"No, that is nice of you but I will return to my duties, it was just a little hiccup, I can carry on - thank you Tom; I shall inform Jerry that you were magnificent in my time of need." Beryl smiled thankfully and returned to her charity work.

Tom heaved the fallen man to his feet, as he was showing signs of recovery and, forcibly man-handled him to the police station. After the full gist of the day's events were reported, Vince was held in custody momentarily whilst he was investigated. He did not divulge that he was working for anybody in particular, only that he was frustrated at not being given the directions he was seeking. As he had a clean slate, Vince was allowed the benefit of the doubt and he was set free. He was told to leave the district or be detained again.

Vince went to his vehicle and waited to see what time Beryl knocked off, when she did; he followed her. He did not get far as another vehicle pulled over between the two cars; it was driven by Tom. He quickly alighted and accosted Vince.

"What the bloody hell do you think you are doing?" Vince angrily shouted.

"My duty!"

Tom returned as he opened the door of Vince's vehicle and dragged the man from it.

"You will stop following that young lady and get out of the district, or else you will feel the weight of my anger upon you - is that understood?"

Tom shook the rather heavy man as though he were a kitten and threw him to the ground. Vince got up with much speed and made a grab for the glove-box of his car. Tom pre-empted the move and again dragged Vince out and gave him a couple of vicious body chops. Vince lay beaten upon the ground.

By this time Beryl had gone, all unaware of the melodrama being enacted behind her. She continued to the mansion and home, quite safely.

Tom went to the beaten man's vehicle and looked into the glove-box to see what it was that Vince was striving to acquire; it proved to be a hand gun. Tom carefully placed it in his handkerchief without contaminating the weapon with his own D.N.A.; and again escorted Vince to the local constabulary.

This time he requested to see his other friend Detective John Mann.

"Yes Tom, what is the problem? Hello, you have brought me a visitor; what is the trouble?" He looked with interest at the man whom Tom escorted.

"This chap I brought in a while ago for accosting a friend of mine and he was let go with a warning, now I caught him following the lady he accosted and we had a bit of a scuffle, he tried to get at this weapon in his glove box but I pre-empted the move and threw him to the ground. I carefully put the gun in a clean handkerchief and brought him in again. His vehicle should be looked at by you people, you never know what you may find; it is parked near the bend at Rafferty's corner!" Tom smiled at the expression on John Mann's face.

"Do you want this man charged?" The detective asked.

"I do not know if a charge will stick, after all I did man-handle him for self protection. If he is not licensed for the firearm, he could be held for that; I just need for him to not bother my clients!" Tom was adamant.

Vince spoke up.

"Okay, I do have a permit for the pistol, I need it in my work as a licensing officer. I will leave the district and go back to the city. Can I go now?"

"We will verify your entitlement to have the weapon and if you are cleared, then I do advise you to do as suggested and clear out of the district - understood?" John Mann looked severely at the desperado.

Chapter Six

Beryl arrived home to the happy face of Jerry, who happened to be coming down the path towards the fernery of the mansion.

"Well now, how did your day go Beryl, was it to your liking?"

"Oh! Pretty good, there was just a slight hiccup but otherwise I rather enjoyed the experience. I do thank you for introducing me to those people - they really are a great bunch of folk who greeted me with open arms and I was just another volunteer. It will be a rather enjoyable pastime for me and I really do like to mix it with the locals; they are a nice lot and it is truly an eye-opener for me!"

Beryl was bubbling over with happiness which belied the little hiccup.

"Now just what was this little hiccup?"

"Oh, nothing really, I suppose I had best tell you in case someone else does. There was a stranger who came in and he was enquiring after you, he would not take no as an answer. He wanted to know where you lived, of course I was not about to tell him so he grabbed me and dragged me out of the shop. Then your private bodyguard came to my assistance and threw him down. I believe he warned the man to get out of the district - that is all! I do not think he will bother us again."

Beryl smiled as if it was just a mundane matter.

Jerry's raised eyebrows showed a great deal of worry.

"Who was the man - do you know?"

"No, Tom took him away; perhaps he knows more. If I see him again I will ask him for you shall I?" Beryl herself raised her eyebrows.

"It is all right Beryl, he will report the matter to me in time. Did the incident shake you up at all, it did not frighten you away from charity work - did it?" Jerry showed genuine concern which made Beryl feel very safe.

"No, not at all, I used to get mixed up with that sort of situation quite often in my past; I am used to desperadoes and that sort of thing. Rest easy, I am tougher than you may think!" Beryl grinned.

Jerry could see that the experience meant little to his lady and bowed to her knowledge of the seedy side of her past existence. He fervently hoped that it was indeed now her past existence, for she definitely was becoming a lady of refinement as he hoped she would become. He grunted contentedly.

They retired to the mansion for an 'after work' breather and a glass of cool drink whilst they reminisced about mundane matters, the evening meal would not be ready for an hour or so; Jerry used the break to gently coax from Beryl a little more of this stranger who accosted her. Since the advent of his association with Beryl, the underworld had cropped up and as an astute businessman, Jerry wanted to glean all he could about any strange oddments that happened which could lead to an interruption to his business enterprises.

To this end, Jerry found it very frustrating that he had to await a report from his bodyguard. He did not wish to divert Beryl from her attentions to the finer points of becoming a lady, she would find that hard enough to cope with and any other diversions would only complicate things for her.

The dinner gong gently sounded and all attended the lavish meal that was set before them. After Beryl had retired to her bedroom with a book that she was reading, one that she had obtained from the charity organisation; Jerry had a secret meeting with his bodyguard who rang earlier to arrange the event.

"Well Tom, I have been on tenter-hooks to hear all about this stranger who accosted Beryl; do you know him at all - did you get a name?"

Jerry was eager to find out what Tom had to report.

"No, I did not know him and enquiries have not led to anything in the district. He is a stranger to this district but my friend at the police station, John Mann, has made some inroads about him - and do you know what - he works for this Olly Quinton who has connections with the thugs that are bothering my clients! His name is Vince Price (something to do with licensing) and he has connections to the big wigs of marketing - this could be the lead we have been looking for - it may give us an insight into Olly's infrastructure."

"Did you get any information at all of why he is in this area?"

"Other than to find you I have no idea, unless Olly sent him to check you out as an opposition to his own business."

"No, it would not be that, somehow this Olly Quinton has cottoned on to the fact that Beryl has connections to me; I am almost certain that he is after Beryl. This Vince evidently does not know Beryl or he would have recognised her at the charity place. How they knew Beryl is here has got me puzzled though!"

"Would Beryl have let anything slip out? You know she is only new to this place, she might have inadvertently spoken to someone and unwittingly given something of her past life away!" Tom pouted.

"No, Beryl is very cagey, she is an astute girl and her knowledge of the rat-bags in the city communities gives her an advantage; Beryl would not fall for that sort of caper! Olly has somehow learned of her whereabouts and is seeking revenge, he does not like to be bettered by a female. You see Tom, Beryl absconded with one of Olly's hirelings limousines and he is after revenge. That is why I needed her to be looked after, Beryl is in grave danger!"

"Gosh Mister Thorn-dyke, no wonder you enlisted my services; not to worry, I shall keep a sharp lookout for you both - never fear - that is my forte!"

"Yes I know Tom, thank you for your diligence and for keeping me informed. Are you letting the authorities know what has transpired?"

"All serene there, they need an undercover agent and are grooming me for that purpose; so I regularly have to report in to them." Tom grinned.

Vince arrived back at the home of Olly Quinton where he was greeted with a surly look.

"Well, what did you find out?"

His employer asked, he had been given bad news. The word around the traps was that he was being investigated.

"Ran into a spot of bother up there, this Thorn-dyke bloke has a heavy on the prowl all the time; Karate Master or some such. He is a serious threat to any one trying to nose about. I did find a lady at a charity shop who knows Thorn-dyke pretty well, trouble is she is very cagey and refused to tell me anything. I never saw any street tart at all, I do not reckon he would tolerate a girlie up at his mansion." Vince shook his head, convinced he was right.

"Look, the bitch was with the chauffeur and she was all prizzied up, are you sure the lady you spoke to wasn't the one I am looking for? I don't think she will look like a street girl now, Thorn-dyke has probably had her all done up to fit in; that Sheila you spoke to might have been her!" Olly frowned.

"Nah! The person I asked was a lady, she wasn't no street girl."

"Ah! Forget the bitch for now, I got troubles here to cope with. A very large consignment has been allocated to me to have processed and ready for the streets, a good portion of it I have prearranged for the heavies and they are eagerly awaiting its distribution. Gruen Hughes wants that lot and Jonno will deliver that from my cutting room when it is processed. What I need from you is to get the stuff that will be for the streets, when it is ready and until Slugger is cleared, I need for you to take over his duties. The bloody dick-heads of coppers have already landed him for that lot and will be watching him all the time. You are a new face and I am informed by my sources that you are in the clear so far as the authorities know. You should have no trouble with the pick-up, see that you keep it that way. Even the stinking Feds are nosing about now so be on your guard. Think you can handle it?"

Olly glared at his servant as if daring him to refuse.

"No worries, she's Jake!" Vince smugly went about his duties.

Tom was reporting the latest knowledge of his intervention with Vince to the higher ranks of the squad that was investigating Olly Quinton.

Captain Smerdon, the co-ordinator of the squad had heard all about Tom's introduction to Vince and his apparent interest in Jerry Thorn-dyke's relationship with the lady from the Charity Shop.

"So now Jerry thinks that Olly is seeking his lady friend does he? Sending a 'heavy' for the purpose is really strange, did Jerry say why this Olly, a suspected drug dealer, wants to find his lady friend?" Captain Smerdon asked.

"From what I have gathered, she evidently absconded with the limousine when one of Olly's henchmen picked her up from the Casino; she was in the dining room and had gone to the ladies room when she was snatched. She took his 'limo' when he alighted and she scrambled into the driving seat and sped off, it was abandoned at a taxi rank I am informed." Tom smiled at the fact.

"Ah yes, I do believe one of the officers reported that incident, he told the squad about it as the vehicle is registered to Olly. So that's how it got there! So Olly is after the lady to get even with her. This could add to his convictions when we do get something solid on him - good. Thank you Tom, you look like becoming an asset to us - oh! I have some good news for you, you have passed our safety check and can be sworn in as an agent. So do you want to abide by your word? If so, then please be sworn in as a temporary agent!"

Captain Smerdon had an engulfing grin as he shook hands expectantly.

Tom was given his rights and responsibilities, then duly sworn in as an agent.

Jerry Thorn-dyke was speaking to his legal practitioner.

"So as my lady friend has apparently left her past behind her and is now on the road to becoming a lady of substance, that past will not adversely affect our future will it; I mean, is there a chance that she could be detrimental to any of my business enterprises? I know that if I do make her my wife she will inherit a good deal of my fortune, how do I safeguard myself?"

"Yes, the legal formalities must be thoroughly looked at, there are ways that you may safeguard yourself; I shall peruse the matter carefully for you Mister Thorn-dyke!" The legal man pouted as he nodded thoughtfully.

"Thank you Mister Bannister, I will leave it to you then?"

Jerry waved as he smiled his thanks and left.

Vince had just picked up that minor parcel of 'goods' for Olly Quinton and was taking the small shipment to Olly's house, he did not know that he was being monitored by two under cover policemen. They watched through binoculars as he took the goods into the luxurious home of his boss. It would be detrimental to their investigations to raid the premises now just for this one small shipment, as they had been briefed, 'let this one go for it may lead to something bigger'. There will be enough evidence in the house for a later conviction, 'we must confirm the connection between Olly and the importer!'

The two under cover agents remained out of sight and kept an alert eye upon the now known house, where a contraband transaction was taking place.

Detective John Mann was in earnest conversation with his new confidant, Tom Mand, they were discussing the information that had been passed down from the head of 'The Phoenix Squad'.

"Now if you do come across this 'Vince' any where near Mister Thorn-dyke or his lady friend Beryl, we will need to know immediately - that is an order right from the top. We have two of our men keeping a sharp eye upon him at the moment but we do not want them to blow their cover if Vince does happen to be sent after Beryl again. They are aware of your connections to our cause and have been informed to leave matters to you if he does approach her again. We need to keep the underworld ignorant of them and your connection with us - is that clear?" John Mann gave Tom a severe look.

"Yes John, very clear and I am proud that the 'powers that be' have seen fit to let me have a little leeway. I will do everything according to the law!"

Beryl was once again at her post as a volunteer at the Charity Shop. Vera Collins welcomed her with a huge smile.

"Oh it is going to be a glorious day, I do hope that people will flock to the shop and make us busy; the more that we can sell the better for our cause!"

She fluttered about opening up the premises and adjusting this and that for a better display.

"Yes Vera, it will be nice if the population do visit us and with the weather in our favour, I see no reason why we cannot amass a nice sum for our cause. Er, which cause are we actually sponsoring?" Beryl was very interested.

"We do assist various struggling concerns, one is the local children's hospital, then there is the aged care home and also we do try to amass a fair lump of our gains for Christmas time. It is amazing just how strapped for cash the Salvation Army gets around the festive season; our little dribble assists all of those concerns and we try to be fair to them all!"

Her engulfing grin made Beryl smile for she could see how keen Vera was for those causes.

"Well with such a champion as a leader I know that I have made the right choice in volunteering." Beryl happily asserted.

"You will see, the more you give then the more you will be happy with that choice, goodness knows; we are forever needing staff as the people who donate of their time for us are usually the ones that have the most responsibilities. Nearly all of the volunteers have young families of their own and that is why we often run out of staff; they get all sorts of hiccups at home which they need to attend as an emergency. I was so pleased when I learned that Mister Thorn-dyke had sent you, you are more or less a free spirit!"

"Ah! Here we go, the first customer is approaching. I remember Dorothy from yesterday, I recognise that beat up trolley that she always uses for a crutch. There are many of our customers that use us as a community welfare centre, they always seem to buy an oddment or two; I guess it is just their way of donating to charity." Beryl observed.

As the morning progressed and people continually browsed through the shop, Beryl was kept busy with people and did not take much notice of Slugger who was peering through the front window. He was hard for her to recognise as he had a large sombrero type hat upon his head that concealed his features well and a pair of sun glasses, therefore he was unnoticed by Beryl who would have known him immediately if she had not been so busy with customers. Slugger did not enter the premises and when he recognised Beryl, he was amazed at her transformation. His desire was to go and get Beryl but his instructions were to just see if indeed the lady at the charity shop was Beryl. Having ascertained that this was so, he left to report back to his boss.

Back at Olly's house, Slugger was affirming that it really was that smart-arsed bitch who took his 'Limo'. Still fuming he was listening to his boss.

"So, she's been transformed into a lady eh! Well a leopard can't change it's spots, she is still a bloody tramp. Now wait a bit until I come up with a plan, we don't want you to be getting caught up with that Martial Arts guy, I can't afford to have the cops get involved; we got too much going to be getting mixed up in a scandal. Vince got lumbered because the stupid prick thought snatching the girl was like a walk in the park, this guy what's got hold of her is a big nob in society and we gotta do this properly. He evidently has a bunch of his own 'heavies' guarding the Sheila. I will think of some way to do this right. You have to be careful 'cos you are probably being monitored too!"

Slugger just nodded and went about his duties.

Tom Mand had completed his commitments for the Saturday at his Karate Centre and after speaking to his wife, decided that the afternoon would be a good time to check up on his ward at the Charity Shop. Week-ends were a busy time for the staff and although Tom and Jane were well known to most of the staff, they mingled with the other customers virtually unnoticed. The two martial arts people thought it best to not linger in there too long, so they decided to go next door and have a latte. A smart looking limousine pulled up outside the cafe' where they were idly gossiping and they gave it just a casual glance, often these upper class vehicles were to be seen at the little township; so of course it was not unusual to witness another. The lady and gentleman from the classy limo' casually walked across the road to the local pub and entered. The two watching took little notice of the couple thinking that they were just out for a casual drink, possibly to spend an hour or two relaxing. Tom informed Jane that Beryl had finished her shift and was leaving to go home, when they noted that the people from the limo' were also coming to their vehicle. They were walking quickly and watching Beryl enter her little car. Warning bells clanged in Tom's mind as they too, went to their own car. As Beryl motored home they were followed by the couple in the limousine. Tom and Jane kept both of the other vehicles in sight, awaiting what may occur. Beryl approached a quiet lane prior to the road that led to the mansion when the limo' sped past and blocked her further progress. The couple alighted and approached Beryl.

"Excuse me Miss!" The man smiled. "Would you be Beryl?"

"Who wants to know?" Beryl answered.

"We are friends of Jerry Thorn-dyke and were sent by him to inform you that there has been a change of plans; he had to go to the city urgently and would like you to accompany him. We were sent to take you to him!"

Beryl became very suspicious and used her mobile to ring Missus Simpson for verification. The man opened her car door and dragged her out.

"There is no need to ring, you must come with us!"

As Beryl struggled with the two the car driven by Tom came to a dusty stop and before it had come to the standstill, Jane was racing to Beryl's defence.

Throwing the woman aside she smartly chopped the man in the stomach and then delivered a throat chop. He fell to the ground gasping as Jane centred her attention upon the lady; who had scrambled to her feet and aimed a pistol at Jane. Unnoticed by her, Tom had managed to get behind her when she was upon the ground and chopped the pistol away from her. He firmly held the female by the wrist and demanded to know who sent them.

"Mind your own bloody business!" She screamed.

Jane walked up to them and quietly said.

"Leave her to me Tom, I will make her speak or she will regret it; it takes a female to squeeze this sort of toad!"

Her quiet demeanour frightened the miscreant.

"A bloke offered us a quantity of 'snort' if we took her to him. He reckons she is just a tart he used one-time and she nicked off with his limo', he wants revenge. It's no big deal!" The lady muttered.

"When you pointed a pistol at my lady you may just as well have pointed it at me. I am making a citizen's arrest and anything you say may be used against you in a court of law."

The two were taken to the police station and Detective Mann was left the responsibility of charging the two with attempted kidnapping and being in possession of an unlicensed firearm. After much dialogue it was found that the person who offered the 'quantity of 'snort'; was Olly Quinton. The flustered couple, when they realised the enormity of what the job they attempted was leading to; came clean and were urged to attest against Olly Quinton. This they willingly agreed to with a reduction in their charges.

When Beryl related this last attempt to abduct her to Jerry, he was appalled at the audacity of this rogue 'Olly'; how he got wind of Beryl's whereabouts was the conundrum.

"I am sorry Beryl but I guess your association to me and your 'safe haven' is now blown wide open, not to worry, you are quite safe within the grounds of my mansion. I am afraid you will have to give away your charity work though; it is not worth the risk now. When this Olly is finally collared by the authorities you will be a safe and free agent again. Until then it is better that you keep within the bounds of the mansion. Tom is proving his worth to me, gosh I am glad that he decided to monitor you on Saturday. You say that Jane accosted the woman? My word those two are an asset all right, I am so relieved that I have them!" Jerry smiled contentedly.

They adjourned to the house and had a quiet discussion over drinks.

Back at the 'Phoenix' headquarters, Superintendent Hallam Hoskins was in urgent conversation with Captain Smerdon, co-ordinator of the squad.

"Now we have a solid case against this Olly Quinton and can tie in the big nob's if this raid goes as planned. Through our intelligence agencies we have been able to affirm that a certain 'Tomas Barrington' - exporter - is the head of the cartel that is shipping the drugs in - he is being covered by our overseas branch - the importer is this Olly Quinton and he is selling to a 'Gruen Hughes'! Now Olly has another huge consignment coming and this one we had better make sure that we do intercept. Got that? There will be no slip-ups what-so-ever, this has to be a very smooth operation and each squad will abide strictly by the rules. It is mainly through the intervention of this young lady of the streets, that we have made the connection of Olly to the networks. We can not afford to let this opportunity pass us by; get to it chaps and good hunting. If all goes well then we should be able to clean up at least this one cartel." The raids were outstanding successes and a complete stop was put to Olly's branch!

When Tom Mand was notified of the complete success in stopping Olly Quinton, and the fact that he was now in police custody, a very satisfied smile was upon his face. Tom arranged a meeting with his benefactor.

"The good news Sir, is that now your prodigy can return to her social activities without fear of again being accosted by any 'stand-over' thugs. I shall occasionally keep an eye upon her safety, however things will be very different from now on Mister Thorn-dyke. Will that be all for now Sir?"

"Tom, you have eased a very large burden from my mind; thank you and your wife too - I will see that a bonus is forthcoming for you both!"

"Oh no Sir, it is a pleasure to be of assistance. There is no need -?"

He was cut off mid-sentence.

"Yes there is a need, you jumped immediately that I called, the bonus stands and once again; from the bottom of my heart - thank you again!"

Beryl had been told of the arrests and complete eradication of at least this one cartel and her heart was pounding at the look of relief upon Jerry's face as he told her.

"Oh! So I can once more venture out in the freedom of the country air and get deeply involved with my charity work? What a most pleasant relief, we should celebrate! At last my future seems to have blossomed, I do so admire these country folk who have shown me nothing but respect and friendship. I am really beginning to live now - thank you so much for rescuing me Jerry."

"Ah piffle, I saw that deep down there was a lady of substance within that beautiful body, you are more than proving that my perceptions were right; yes we will celebrate; I shall take you out to the best restaurant in our little community and we will most certainly enjoy our own company this evening!"

THE END